THE LEGEND OF JAKE JACKSON

BOOK TWO

A WESTERN ADVENTURE

WILLIAM H. JOINER JR.

DEDICATION

Gerald Red Elk, old friend and
former high school classmate

ACKNOWLEDGEMENTS

I am grateful for the constant support of my wife, Tina, and my children, Jacob, Caleb, Sarah and Ainslee.

Thank you to Missy Brewer for editing this book, to Michael Campbell for the book design, and to Bryan Gehrke for the cover artwork.

John 14:6 Jesus answered, "I am the way and the truth and the life. No one comes to the Father except through me."

A NOTE FROM
BESTSELLING AUTHOR
ROBERT HANLON

Those who have had the pleasure of reading the great Westerns Bill Joiner writes—yes I know—many of you already know what I am going to say. Those who have had the pleasure—well let me just cut it short and tell you that he has a great style you'll love. Joiner, to me, is one of those writers who can really get a story across to his audience. He has drive. He's a driven writer—and you'll love this one. It's called "The Legend of Jake Jackson" and it's the kind-of story you've been asking for. Action, gunplay and lots of story. Grab it!

Robert Hanlon – author of the bestselling "<u>Timber: United States Marshal</u>" series, and many other Western adventures.

A NOTE FROM BESTSELLING AUTHOR

JOHN D. FIE, JR.

Well… what can I say other than give this one a shot! It's the latest, and greatest from the talented Mister Joiner.

Jake Jackson's real family gets killed by a warring Indian party. He is raised by the Indians and becomes a celebrated warrior. Disaster strikes when the Comanche are moved to a reservation. I won't tell you the rest—but our hero becomes mighty good with a gun.

Heck—forget my blathering! Just read the book!

John D. Fie, Jr. – author of the bestselling "Gunfighter" series, and many other Western adventures.

The Legend of Jake Jackson

Jake couldn't help but smile when he saw the familiar 6666 brand. It felt good to get back to north Texas. As he neared the big house at the ranch headquarters, some of the cowboys stopped what they were doing to watch him. When he dismounted to tie his horse at the hitching rail, a voice boomed out from behind the screen door, "Good God Almighty! Look what the cat dragged up!"

Burk Burnett bounded through the door and off the porch. He grabbed Jake in a bear hug and pounded his back. Burk exclaimed, "Where you been, boy? I wondered if I'd ever see you again!" Jake laughed, "It's good to see you too, old friend! I didn't know if I'd ever be back, but here I am!"

Burk eyeballed the big buckskin stud, "Jake, you always had an appreciation of good horseflesh. Where'd you get that beast?" Jake replied, "You mean ol' Buck? Found him." Burk furrowed his brow, "You either bought him or stole him. Which was it?" Jake grinned, "Neither! Like I said, I found him. He was running a herd of mares in the Davis Mountains. It took me two weeks to catch him. It was another two weeks to get him to the point where I could touch him without being bitten or kicked. Buck is the gamest horse I've ever had. No matter how tired he gets, he won't quit me." Burk raised an eyebrow, "I ain't never seen a mustang his equal…not even close."

Burk put an arm around Jake's shoulders, "Come on in the house. I'll have Cookie rustle us up some grub." Jake responded, "That sounds good. I'm hungry enough to eat a buzzard's leavings. Let me put Buck in a stall and feed

1

him." Burk interjected, "I'll have one of my men do it." Jake replied, "Not if you're planning on keeping your man alive. Buck won't tolerate anyone but me touching him. I never worry about him being stolen. That would be one horse thief you wouldn't have to hang. The only problem would be finding his head to bury with the body. I'll warn your men about not touching him. It wouldn't hurt if you told them too."

Over supper, Jake asked, "How is Quanah Parker doing these days? Is he well?" Burk responded, "Quanah is doing real good. He made a lot money leasing me Indian land to graze my cows. He's given up teepee living. Quanah built himself a nice house west of Ft. Sill. Dang Comanche is one of the richest Indians alive!" Jake was glad that Quanah had done well. He also knew that despite his bluster, Burk Burnett and Quanah Parker were great friends.

When Jake went to visit, Quanah greeted him by his Comanche name, "It is good to see my friend, White Wolf. Come inside. We will smoke." Quanah asked, "You look well. How has the white man treated you?" Jake took a drag from the pipe and said, "I have found that the white man and the red man are similar. There are good and bad in both people." It did Jake's heart good to see a number of Quanah's grandchildren playing around the house.

The Next Day

The next day Burk asked Jake, "Do you need any money or a job? I got both." Jake shook his head, "I've got a little money from past jobs. Punching cows is a good honest living. I'm just not interested in doing that anymore." Burk responded, "We heard a lot of stories about you in the last few years. Some of them were hard to swallow. What are you interested in doing?" Jake heard the same stories. There were a few that were exaggerated, others were not. Jake didn't bother to confirm or deny. One thing life had taught him was if it doesn't matter, why bother?

Jake thought for a minute before answering, "I only accept a job if it interests me and I can see it helps someone who can't help themselves. Most can't do what I do." Burk replied, "Yeah, I remember. I have been having a small problem with thieves rustling my cattle. Would you be interested in trying to stop them?" Jake nodded his head, "Burk, you know I would help you in whatever you needed. I'll go into Wichita Falls tomorrow and nose around a bit. See what folks are saying about rustlers."

Stephen Ransom was a lawyer in Wichita Falls. His shingle brought in a lot of business mainly because of the scarcity of attorneys in north Texas. What none of his clients knew that while the law degree diploma hanging on his wall from Yale was genuine, Ransom had fled Boston one step ahead of the police. The Boston police were wanting to question Ransom regarding an illegal stock deal that had gone belly up.

Not long after arriving in Wichita Falls, Ransom became friends with Yancey Yoder. Yoder came to Ransom asking for legal advice. Basically, Yoder wanted to know how he could hoodwink another ranch owner out of his property. After successfully instructing Yoder on how he could navigate the legal system to screw his neighbor out of his ranch, Ransom and Yoder became fast friends.

One day over coffee at an upscale restaurant, Yoder asked, "Ransom, you interested in making some money? I'm not talking about the pittance you collect in legal fees. I'm talking about making some real money!" Ransom grinned, "I guess I need to go up on my legal fees, especially to you!...Seriously, I'm always interested in making money. What do you have in mind?"

Yoder lowered his voice, "A lot of these small ranchers are struggling right now. I suspect there's a bunch of them behind on their taxes. The problem? Most of those behind aren't forced to auction unless someone specifically files wanting to claim the property. That's land that can be bought pretty damn cheap. I can use that land to expand my cattle operation. If I had to pay market price, I couldn't afford it. I need you to search the courthouse records and force tax sales. You would be my partner."

Ransom stroked his chin in thought. He exclaimed, "There's one little hole in your bucket. Those auctions are public. Anybody can bid on them. The prices could easily go back to market value." Yoder replied, "I've already thought about that. If someone want to bid on a tax auction, they have to register 48 hours in advance. Me and my boys will see to it that anybody who registers won't be at the auction."

Ransom asked, "How are you going to keep people from going to the auction?" Yoder smirked, "You needn't concern yourself with that. That's my end of the business." Ransom didn't ask any more questions. He figured what he didn't know wouldn't hurt him.

Sheriff Otis Taylor knocked on the old farm house door. When Ben Johnson answered the door, he was surprised to see the Sheriff, "Why Sheriff Taylor, what are you doing here? I ain't seen you in a coon's age!" Martha interrupted her husband, "Ben Johnson, where are your manners?...Sheriff Taylor, please come in and sit a spell. I'll make us a pot of coffee."

Sheriff Taylor hung his head. He was obviously uncomfortable, "No ma'am, I can't do that. I'm here on official business." Ben was puzzled, "Official business? Official business? What in tarnation would that be?" The Sheriff sighed, "I got to post your place for auction to satisfy the back taxes." Ben exploded, "Otis, me and you go back a long way! Why would you do that?" Sheriff Taylor frowned, "It don't got nothing to do with you and me, Ben. I don't have a choice. The law says there's going to be an auction in two weeks to satisfy the tax bill. I got no say in it."

Ben heavily sat down in the old rocker on the porch. He was speechless. Martha asked, "Sheriff, what can we do?" The Sheriff replied, "Ma'am, the only thing you can do is pay the outstanding taxes due on your place." Martha responded, "We owe for three years. We don't have that kind of money. Is there not anything else we can do or try?" Sheriff Taylor said, "You might try to sell out before the auction. That would pay your taxes and leave y'all some left over."

Ben looked up from his chair, "Forget it...Martha, I ain't told you because I didn't want you to be upset. I done checked around with our neighbors. They ain't got no money either. It's what they call 'cash poor.' We got land, but no cash."

Sheriff Taylor brightened, "Well, maybe they'll be a bunch of folks at the auction bidding on the place. You might come out good that way." Ben muttered, "How can it be good when we're gonna lose our land?"

After Sheriff Taylor returned to Wichita Falls, tears rolled down Martha's cheeks. She sobbed, "Oh Ben, what are we going to do? Where are we going to go?" Ben shrugged, "I don't know, dear. I never seen this coming. I always figured whenever we got on in years that we'd be comfortable. Working all these years should have counted for something. Instead, we won't even have a home. We'll be flat broke."

Martha suggested, "Rayanne and her husband are doing well with their café in Bridgeport. I know she would help us." Ben snorted, "We ain't doing that! I got a little pride left. I'm not sponging off our daughter. Whatever happens, we'll deal with it."

The Banker

Banker Raymond Wheeler made sure he received all notifications from the courthouse. He felt like he needed to know everything that might affect the bank or its customers. When Wheeler read of the Johnson place being posted for auction, he thought, "I know where that is. That's a nice piece of property. I think I'll will go by the courthouse today to register as a bidder." Some might wonder why Wheeler would acquire the land in his name instead of the Bank's? Wheeler always put the Bank's interests ahead of its customers' interests. He never put anything or anybody ahead of his own interests.

That night Wheeler worked late as he usually did. His wife complained that he was never at home, "Raymond, why is it you always have "pressing" work at the bank that can't wait till the next morning? You've got two kids who I doubt even know what their father looks like! Are you seeing another woman? I'll bet it's one of those floozies from the Red Dog Saloon!"

Wheeler replied, "Don't be ridiculous, Susan. I'm just trying to keep a roof over our heads and clothes on our backs." He thought, "Why would I want to come home to a nag and two squalling brats? If I can get enough cash put back, I'm taking that bank manager's job that was offered me out in San Francisco. Leaving you and those joy-swillers will be the happiest day of my life."

The banker heard a noise. He peered out of the door to his office. Wheeler saw a dark shadow. When the shadow moved into the light of the moon coming in a window, the banker recognized him. Wheeler demanded, "Yoder, why are you here? You know the bank is closed. How did you even get in here?...If this is about your loan request that was denied, my decision still stands. You are not a reliable risk that the bank is willing to take!"

Yoder laughed, "Actually, Raymond, that's not why I'm here at all." Wheeler visibly flinched at Yoder being so familiar, "See here, Yoder! Have you taking leave of your senses? It is now and always will be Mr. Wheeler to you!

You are starting to annoy me. If you're not out of here in two minutes, I will be forced to notify the police!"

Yoder continued to grin, "You just don't get it, do you RAYMOND? The police can't help you now. The only one who can help you is the undertaker!" Wheeler watched in horror and disbelief as flames shot out of the end of the barrel of the sixgun clutched in Yoder's hand. The first bullet slammed into Wheeler's chest, an inch above his heart. The second punctured an eye, exiting out of the back of his skull. Yoder smirked and stood for a moment admiring the twitching body of the banker before hurrying out the side door.

Yoder's next stop was the shack where the janitor lived who he had paid to leave the door unlocked. The janitor had the same incredulous look on his face as Wheeler had. Yoder shot him to death, "Sorry, oldtimer, I can't afford to have any loose ends."

Sheriff Taylor scratched his head as he said to his deputy, "There ain't no clues and there's a hundred people who would have liked to see Raymond Wheeler dead. His widow weren't no help neither. I expected tears and hysterics like I usually get when I tell a women that her husband has been killed. When I told her, all she said was 'When do I get his money?' Have you ever heard of the like?"

Yoder and two of his henchmen watched the rider come up the road to the old ranch house. Yoder stood up, "Ransom, what are you doing out here?" Ransom grimly said, "We need to talk...alone." Yoder motioned for his men to go to the barn. Ransom stated, "Yoder, I didn't agree to no killings. I want out of our deal!"

Yoder sat back down on the old chair, "Well how in the hell did you think I was going to eliminate our competition at the auctions? Ask them real polite like? This ain't back east, counsellor. We do things a little different out here. And you ain't backing out of our deal! If you try it, you might find yourself in a plot right next to Wheeler on boot hill! My suggestion would be to keep your mouth shut and enjoy the money...One other thing, if you ever come out here again, I'll kill you!"

Taylor

Sheriff Taylor sighed and took a deep breath before knocking on the Johnson's door. When Ben opened it, Taylor thrust a piece of paper at him, "Ben, I'm real sorry about this. The only one who showed up at the auction was one of those damn lawyers. He only bid enough to pay the taxes. That is the eviction notice to vacate within two weeks. Damn, I'm sorry."

Ben smiled at the Sheriff as he put out his hand to shake, "Otis, it weren't you fault. You're only following the law. Tell the new owner he won't have to wait two weeks. I can't bear to be here no more. Me and Martha will be out tomorrow at sunup."

When the dawn broke the next day, Ben hooked up the old slab-sided mule to the rickety wagon packed with their meager belongings. He slapped the reins, "Gittup, Chester. We're headed to Bridgeport. Maybe Rayanne will give me a job washing dishes." Martha cried for a bit before slipping her hand into her husband's. She gave it a squeeze to let him know they were going to be alright.

Ransom gave some thought to sneaking out of town, but thought better of it. He said to himself, "I probably could slip out like I did in Boston, but I already got a decent practice built up. I wouldn't want to leave that behind and start over. I do have a snake for a partner, but I have to admit we're going to make good money buying these farms and ranches at tax sales. When I get enough saved back, I can always leave then…or I could maybe hire a killer to take care of my partner…Yeah, that would be better than leaving all this money."

Yancey Yoder stretched and grinned at his two gunhands, "Well, I guess it's a waste of time to ask the two of you to do any actual work tending to our herd." Jesse replied, "Yancey, you knowed what you hired us for. It wasn't following behind these stinking cows. We don't mind handling a branding iron now and then. You pay us to handle our shooting irons." Billy confirmed, "Boss, you can bring on cow punchers all day. Regulators like me and Jesse are hard to come by."

Yoder laughed, "It's a good thing I got a real foreman to ramrod that bunch in the bunkhouse otherwise I'd have cattle scattered all over hell and gone. With this new place I just acquired, we're gonna need some more livestock. I got about a month before I buy another place. In the meantime the three of us is gonna mosey out west Texas way to buy cows." They all knew when Yancey said "buy" he meant "steal."

There weren't many old timers like Gus Daniels left anymore. He had carved out a small ranch just east of Pecos with nothing but his sweat and nerve. Gus had dealt with hostile Indians, rustlers and the unrelenting heat of west Texas. For years Gus considered tumbleweeds as pets to keep from going completely stir crazy. He had a small herd of about 500 cows, steers and bulls. Normally that was a three-man job. Gus did it all by himself.

Yoder snorted, "It looks like just one old man to me. This should be like taking candy from a baby." Jesse replied, "I don't know, Boss. Some of these old codgers are pretty rank. We're gonna have to kill him to take his cows. He may not kill so easy." Billy added, "Hell, it's still just one man. There's three of us. How hard can it be?"

Yoder smirked, "You two girls follow me…and try not to get yourself bitten by that old rattlesnake." The three outlaws rode slowly to the herd. Yoder wanted to appear to be friendly. Gus watched them ride in. He cocked his sixgun just to be careful, but left it in his holster. Yoder held up his hand in greeting, "Howdy, friend. We was thinking about building a small fire and boiling some coffee. You want some?"

Gus looked them over. He didn't like what he saw. Gus growled, "First off, I ain't your friend. I don't need your coffee. I got my own." Yoder laughed, "Whoa, oldtimer. You got us all wrong. We're just trying to be neighborly." Gus responded, "I know all my neighbors. You ain't one. This is my range and my cows. Move on!"

Billy had maneuvered his horse to block Gus's view from seeing him draw his pistol. Billy urged his horse forward. When Gus saw the gun leveled at him, he pulled his own. The bullet from Billy's gun spun Gus around, but Gus kept his seat. Gus returned the gunfire. His slug struck Billy's throat, killing the bandit cleanly.

Yoder shouted, "Kill that sum bitch!" He and Jesse were triggering their own pistols. Gus was hit twice more and finally went down in a heap. Yoder slid off his horse and gingerly turned Gus over with the toe of his boot. Gus was too shot up to live, but he still had a defiant look in his eyes. Yoder stated, "I'll say one thing for you. You are an ornery old coot!" Gus last words were, "Go to hell!"

Yoder mopped the sweat from his forehead with his kerchief, "We got lots of work to do. It's gonna take us two or three days to change the brands to the Circle Y." Jesse nodded towards Billy, "What are we gonna do about him? Bury him?" Yoder frowned, "No we ain't burying that dumb sum bitch. He got hisself kilt. He can get hisself buried."

As they drove the cattle back to the Circle Y, Yoder asked, "Jesse, I need to replace Billy. You know any ol' boys that can handle a gun and don't mind doing it?" Jesse responded, "I been thinking on that some. I know a man who would be perfect for what you would want him for. The problem is he is the jail in Wichita Falls. Supposed to be there another six months. Do you think your lawyer buddy could get him out?" Yoder laughed, "For enough money that shyster would frame his own mama and watch her swing."

Sheriff Taylor turned the key in the cell door lock, "Alright, Nelson. You're out of here! Go on now, git!" Nelson hurried through the open door, "Now, Sheriff, I ain't complaining none, but I thought I was supposed to be in here another six months?" Sheriff Taylor snorted, "You was...until I got this judge's order to release you! I don't know what's going on around here anymore!...If there was ever a coyote who deserved to be in my hoosegow, it's durn sure you! You're lucky that shyster, Ransom found some loophole is some law nobody ever heard of to spring you. He needs to be in a cell too!"

Yoder and Jesse were waiting when Nelson walked out of the jail house. Jesse slapped Nelson on the back and hugged him like they were long lost brothers. Nelson exclaimed, "I thought I was gonna have to serve my time. That dang Sheriff hates me. He wasn't going to give me no break. That's for sure! It wasn't my fault that old lady got hurt. All she had to do was give me her money that I asked for nice and polite. She started giving me a problem so I had to rough her up a bit. But that was on her, not me...old biddy! Thanks for getting me out!"

Jesse nodded toward Yoder, "There's the man you need to thank for getting you out. I told Mr. Yoder you were the type of man who could be real valuable to have around if things got sticky." Nelson stuck out his hand, "I sure thank you, Mr. Yoder. I'll try to repay you one day!" Yoder ignored the handshake, "One day? Hell, you're gonna repay me now!" A startled Nelson sputtered, "I...I...I don't got no money to repay you today!"

Yoder unhitched his horse. As he mounted, Yoder motioned to a horse that was tied next to his, "Get on. Jesse will fill you in on our way back to the ranch…Just remember one thing. I can get you put back in jail just as easy as I got you out!"

Bob and Carol Jenkins were thrilled when they received a registered letter that Carol's uncle left a ranch to Carol in his will. They each reread the letter several times. Bob exclaimed, "All I ever done was clerking in a dry goods store. I reckon I could learn to be a rancher. I mean…how hard could it be?"

Carol was excited, "The lawyer gave the location of the ranch as south of Wichita Falls. Texarkana is the only place I've ever lived, but I'm sure I would like Wichita Falls!" Bob and Carol had been married less than two years, but they were devoted to each other. Bob quit his job. They bought a wagon and a horse. With their worldly goods loaded in it, they struck out for their new lives as wealthy ranchers.

There were frowns on their faces when they surveyed their new home. Finally, Bob spoke, "The old house ain't much, but we can fix it up. The barn and corrals are gonna need repairs too. The good thing is the 500 acres that goes with it!" After looking inside the house, Carol remarked, "I guess it's been a spell since anyone lived here…But, you're right, Bob. We can fix it up!" Bob smiled, "That's my girl!"

The Sheriff's Surprise

The Jenkins were surprised when the Sheriff rode up the next morning. Sheriff Taylor said, "I didn't know anybody lived out here. Do you folks own this place or are you just squatting?" Bob briefly went inside to fetch the letter, "As you can see, Sheriff, me and Carol are the legal owner. We just got here yesterday. Once we get the place in order, we're gonna buy some cattle and become ranchers."

Sheriff Taylor grimaced, "I hate to tell you folks this, but I'm out here today to post this property to sell to satisfy a tax bill. I'm real sorry, but you got two weeks to move out." Carol asked, "It's there anything we can do? Can we pay the back taxes?" Taylor grinned, "Yes ma'am. You go into the courthouse in town. If you pay the taxes, there won't be no sale. The place will be yours free and clear!"

It took most of the money they had saved, but Bob and Carol paid the taxes. When they rode back to their ranch, Bob stated, "Well, we don't have the cash to buy more than a couple of head. It's a start. With a little luck and a lot of hard work, we'll get our ranch going in no time. You'll see!"

Ransom was livid when he was notified that the auction had been cancelled. He had no way of getting word to Yoder of the cancellation. On his way to the café, Yoder motioned him over from an alley. They moved behind the building. Yoder demanded, "What the hell happened?" Ransom replied, "A young couple, Bob and Carol Jenkins, had just inherited the property. They paid the taxes. I had no way to get word to you since you told me not to come back to your place!"

Yoder thought for a minute, "From now on, leave a message at the front desk of your hotel if there's a problem with an auction. The day before I'll send one of my men to pick it up. If there's no message, that means the sale is on…In the meantime I want you to make a bill of sale from this Jenkins deeding me their property. Leave it at the front desk in a sealed envelope. I'll send Jesse to pick it up tomorrow."

Bob and Carol were working diligently repairing and cleaning their house when Yoder rode up with Jesse and Nelson in tow. Yoder waved, "Looks like you folks are hard at it! I would have never figured that old house would ever be livable again." Bob grinned as he wiped his brow, "It's gonna take some work for sure, but we'll get there. Are y'all neighbors?"

Yoder smiled, "We're actually better than neighbors. I'm buying this place." Bob was confused, "Buying?...I don't understand." Yoder continued to smile as he slid off his horse, pulled his pistol and pointed it at Bob, "It's pretty simple. You sign this deed I got and I won't kill you and your pretty wife!" Bob was incredulous, "Surely, you can't be serious! This is our home!"

Yoder said, "Boys." Jesse and Nelson dismounted. They grabbed Carol and forced her on her back. Jesse held her while Nelson lifted her skirts. Bob screamed, "Carol!" as he charged to help his wife. Yoder struck Bob across his forehead with the barrel of his gun, knocking him down. Bleeding from the scalp, Bob rose to one knee, "Please, I'll sign anything…just don't hurt her."

Yoder grinned as he extended the paper and pen. When Bob signed, Yoder blew off most of his head with a slug from his .45. As Carol watched in horror, Jesse asked about the woman, "Boss?" Yoder retorted, "Go ahead but make it quick. We still got to haul off and bury the bodies where no one can find them." When they were finished, Nelson slit Carol's throat. Nelson shrugged as he wiped the blade on her skirt, "I figured no sense in wasting a bullet. Bullets cost money." Yoder nodded his head in agreement.

Jake

Jake introduced himself to Sheriff Taylor, "I'm Jake Jackson." The Sheriff grinned as he shook Jake's hand, "I heard tell of you, but I thought you were dead." Jake smiled, "That's not the first time I've heard that. Sometimes folks get it wrong." Taylor laughed, "How can I help you, Mr. Jackson?"

Jake's eyes narrowed, "I'm doing a little job for Burk Burnett. He's had a small problem with rustlers. I wondered if you can give me any leads that I might check out?" Sheriff Taylor frowned, "Burk's a good man…There are some funny things going on around here. Nothing I can prove, but it's dang sure suspicious. There's a couple of varmints that I think are in cahoots. One is a man named Yoder. He owns a ranch not far from town, the Circle Y. Yoder keeps acquiring ranch land, but there's something about the way he's doing it that smells. I think he's partnered up with a shyster lawyer by the name of Ransom."

The Sheriff paused, "Mr. Jackson, why don't you have a seat and I'll make us a fresh pot of coffee." Jake replied, "I'd like that, but only if you will agree to call me, Jake."

After sipping on the hot coffee, Taylor continued, "I think Yoder and Ransom are working some kind of a deal on property that owes back taxes. I believe Ransom makes it seem legal and Yoder does the dirty work. Just the other day, a young couple, Bob and Carol Jenkins inherited a small ranch. They didn't know there was past taxes due. When I went out to post it for auction, they come into town and paid the taxes. A couple of days later, Yoder shows up with a signed deed from Jenkins. He spouted some cock and bull story about buying it, but he couldn't tell me what happened to Jenkins. Yoder claimed they left. He couldn't even tell me what direction they went. I went out there to see for myself. I didn't find anything."

Jake had been paying close attention. He asked, "Sheriff, could you give me the directions out to that ranch? I'd like to take a look around." Taylor replied, "No problem, but I done looked. I don't think you'll find anything."

Jake's tracking skills were superior to most white men because he had been raised as a Comanche. He learned many things from the Indians that helped him in the white world. It didn't take long before he found their remains. Bob and Carol had been buried in the same grave. Jake had brought along a pack horse equipped with a shovel and several blankets. Jake was confident he would find what he was looking for.

When Jake rode into Wichita Falls leading the horse packing two blanketed bodies, a crowd started following. One man explained, "I'll be durned if that ain't Jake Jackson!" A second man responded, "It can't be him. Everyone knows Jake Jackson has been dead for years!"

After examining the bodies, Sheriff Taylor confirmed they were Bob and Carol Jenkins. He immediately saddled his horse and rode out to the Circle Y. He told Jake, "You're welcome to ride out with me. A trip to the Circle Y might help you put together more pieces to this puzzle. It's looking like I might need all the help I can get."

Yoder grinned, "Why Sheriff Taylor, what brings you out here today?" Yoder extended his hand. Sheriff Taylor ignored it. The Sheriff gruffly said, "Mr. Jackson here, found the bodies of Bob and Carol Jenkins. That don't exactly fit your version of them leaving. What you got to say about that?" Yoder hesitated as he looked over Jake, "You got me. I don't have anything to add to my original statement. They were alive the last time I saw em."

Jake interrupted, "That sounds like a load of buffalo chips to me. Those poor folks were murdered. I think you know who did it!" Yoder replied, "And just who the hell are you? You some kinds lawman?" Taylor responded, "This is Jake Jackson. You may have heard of him. He's sent a passel of outlaws to boot hill. I know I would hate it if Mr. Jackson was on my backtrail. He has a way of getting results when no one else can!"

The tight look on Jesse's and Nelson's faces showed they knew who Jake was. They appeared to be concerned and nervous by the mere presence of Jake. Jesse also began to have a feeling of dread. Yoder announced, "Tell you what, Sheriff. When you or Jackson here get any real proof, come back and see me. Otherwise, stay off my property!"

Jake smiled, "When one of us does come back, you better pray it's the Sheriff and not me. I don't know about the Sheriff, but I can guarantee you I will be back! You may think you've gotten away with all the killing and robbing you've done. You ain't!"

Yoder protested, "Sheriff, that man is threatening me! You're the law. What are you gonna do about it?" Sheriff Taylor replied, "Shut up!"

Later that night when Jake was feeding Buck his oats, he muttered, "Buck ol' boy. I try to be a white man, but sometimes I go back to my Comanche ways. The Comanche have a simple way to handle things. They're not like the white man who has to complicate it. The white man talks too much…writes down too much."

Brooding Over Death

That night Jake brooded on the way Bob and Carol Jenkins died. He could see that Carol had her throat cut and her body was damaged by the assault. The rage in him began to boil. Jake had tried to forget the murder of his wife and their baby. Macy was attacked in the same way as Carol. Macy had suffered the same indignities and atrocities. The old feelings of furious anger rushed to the surface.

Yoder woke up to the specter of a Comanche warrior in full war paint, standing over his bed. A swift blow from the butt of Jake's rifle stifled Yoder's scream. Jake had already incapacitated Jesse and Nelson. They were unconscious, tied and slung over the backs of the horses Jake had brought along for that purpose.

None of the real cowboys on the Circle Y heard anything. All they knew was they woke that morning and their boss and his two henchmen were gone. The cowboys went about their business of tending the cattle. They figured Yoder and his boys would eventually come back. After a week, one of the cowboys asked the rest of the hands, "Mr. Yoder has been gone for quite a while. Do you suppose we should go look for him?" The rest of them looked at the ground, a few shrugged. It was obvious Yoder wasn't missed.

All three men regained consciousness to find themselves stripped naked, staked out and spread-eagled. Yoder stammered, "Wh…Wh…What are you doing? What do you want? This is agin the law!" Nelson began to sob, "Why are you doing this to me? I didn't do nothing except what they made me do! Yoder bailed me out of jail. He said he could put me back in if I didn't do what he wanted!" Jesse was as cold blooded as they come, but even his voice cracked in desperation, "Shut up, Nelson. You took your turn with the woman just like I did…Jackson, I've done some bad things. But, I ain't killed little kids like Yoder done."

Jake heated his knife in the campfire. Try as he might, Jake couldn't control his blood lust. The souls of the man and woman cried out for revenge and justice. Some might say that taking the law in your own hands was not justice. The Comanche side of Jake demanded an eye for an eye.

Jake pulled Nelson's hair away from his scalp. He sliced and jerked at the same time, holding the bloody scalp up for Yoder and Jesse to see. Nelson screamed hysterically. He begged as blood poured down his face into his eyes, "Please kill me! Please kill me!" Jake took the flat side of the hot knife and cauterized the wound. He didn't want Nelson to die too quick. Jake's Comanche sense of justice required that the killers suffered as their victims suffered. Eventually, Nelson became hoarse. His screams were no louder than a dry rasp.

Jesse tried to steel himself against his fate. In the end, his resolve dissolved in begging and pleading. Jesse was also scalped and cauterized. His scalp hung in the tree next to Nelson's. Jesse was as hysterical as his ol' pard, Nelson. Since Jake was not listening, both men begged God for the relief of death.

Yoder was almost insane with horror. He violently twisted against the ropes, but it didn't alter the will of Jake Jackson. Yoder blubbered, "No, no, no, no." It wasn't long before his scalp decorated the same tree where his men's hair hung. Jake had one more punishment for Yoder. Jake carefully and meticulously peeled the skin from the squirming outlaw.

Since the Comanche tribe had been confined to the reservation at Ft. Sill, no Comanche had been seen on the streets of Wichita Falls. Wearing only a breechcloth and still painted for war, Jake rode Buck to the sheriff's office. People were running from shop to shop warning the inhabitants that they were being invaded by a Comanche war party. Someone finally shouted, "That ain't no wild Indian! That's Jake Jackson! I knowed his horse!" Another man exclaimed, "Hell, I'd rather deal with ten Comanche on the warpath than having to deal with Jackson.

Sheriff Taylor's mouth gaped open when Jake walked in his office. Jake threw the three scalps on his desk, "There's your three killers." Jake left without saying another word to

Taylor. The Sheriff didn't move for quite some time. He just stared at the scalps. Jake had one more job to do.

Ransom was in a panic. He had heard that Jake Jackson had brought in the outlaws who killed Bob and Carol Jenkins. Ransom was terror stricken when he was told that Jackson only brought in their scalps. He stuffed all his cash in a bag and caught the next stage headed west.

Ransom craned his neck looking to see if anyone was following. His heart went in his throat when he saw the lone rider approaching. Initially, Ransom was relieved to see that it wasn't an Indian. He was glad to see it was a white man. Ransom's hope was short lived. Jake stopped the stage. He addressed the coach in a clear voice, "Ransom, I know you're in there. I also know you were partners with Yoder. It's time to answer for your crimes. Don't make me come in after you."

The pistol blast was loud and unexpected. Jake cautiously approached the coach with his Colt drawn. He discovered that Ransom had stuck the barrel of a Derringer in his mouth and pulled the trigger. He had preferred a self-inflicted death to facing the justice of Jake Jackson.

She Returns

Eleanor Farnsworth put a finger to her lips to silence her father's secretary. She flung open the door to his office at the Ranchers Bank & Trust and shouted, "Father!" Daniel Farnsworth dropped the pen he was using to sign a document. Not much flustered the old man. That came from having enough money where any and all daily events didn't impact his life.

Farnsworth jumped out from behind his desk in a manner that was unbecoming to the president of a bank. He hugged his daughter tightly, "Eleanor, what in the Sam Hill...How did...What are you doing here?" Eleanor laughed, "I came to see you, silly!" Her father replied, "What about the university?"

Richard had sent his daughter back east to attend a university in Boston. He wanted her to have a proper education. Just as importantly, he wanted her to have a higher class of young men to choose from when it came time for her to marry. Richard frowned at thinking she might marry some rancher or store owner's son in Wichita Falls.

Eleanor continued, "I quit the university. I was sick of the silly classes, sick of the silly people, sick of the silly way they talked! I was even sick of the silly way they dressed! Daddy, I was sick, sick, sick of everything about silly Boston! I missed you. I missed horseback rides. I missed everything about the western way of life! So...here I am!"

Richard responded, "Young lady, you know how I feel about you attending a proper school." Eleanor interrupted, "Father, you may not have noticed, but I am a grown woman! I can make my own decisions!" Richard remembered the effort that was required to send his headstrong daughter off to Boston the first time. He knew sending her back was a losing effort. Richard sighed, "Eleanor, what am I going to do with you?" Eleanor hugged and kissed him, "Why Father, you're going to let me be me!"

Eleanor passed Jake on the wooden sidewalk in front of the café. She twirled her parasol and batted her eyes. Jake tipped his hat and kept walking. Eleanor was a striking beauty. Her looks had always gotten her attention from men and women alike. Being ignored was a new experience for her. She asked a passing woman, "Mrs. Johnson, who is that man?" Mrs. Johnson exclaimed, "My dear, you don't want to know Jake Jackson! He's not fit for civilized company! They say he's done things that will curl your hair and turn your stomach, all at the same time! Miss Farnsworth, it would be best if you steered clear of that man!"

Eleanor couldn't help but keep her gaze on the back of the retreating Jake. She thought, "The turned stomach is not appealing, but the curled hair might be interesting." She stalked the streets of Wichita Falls hoping for another "chance" encounter with Jake. On the third day, Eleanor's pulse quickened at the approach of Jake. Just before their paths crossed. She strategically dropped her purse and exclaimed, "Oh, my!"

Jake bent over to retrieve the purse. He offered it back to Eleanor, "Ma'am." She gave him her biggest smile, "Whoever said chivalry is dead couldn't be more wrong! Not as long as they're gallant men like you around!" Jake wondered why she was making such a fuss over him picking up her purse. Jake replied, "It wasn't anything, ma'am." He went on his way, leaving Eleanor with her mouth half way open as she tried to continue the conversation.

Eleanor was incredulous and frustrated. She stomped one of her little feet and muttered a very unlady-like, "Dammit." When Jake crossed the street to the mercantile, Eleanor loitered outside waiting for him to come out. Jake bought the ammunition he had ordered. When he exited, Eleanor planted herself in front of him as she tapped one of her feet. Jake was puzzled, "Can I help you, ma'am?" Eleanor didn't reply for a few minutes. Finally, she said, "You, sir are a most exasperating man! When a lady is trying to have a conversation with you, a true gentleman would make sure she was finished before leaving!"

Jake took a minute himself before responding. He grinned, "Well ma'am, that was your first mistake. I've been called a lot of things, but a gentleman was never one of them…Now, if you don't mind, I've…" Eleanor cut him off, "See there? That's just what I was talking about. I'm not finished!" Jake laughed, "Okay, okay…Let me be direct. What do you want? Why do you want to talk to me?" Eleanor replied, "Who said I wanted anything? Maybe I just wanted to talk."

Jake sighed, "I admit I can be a little thick when it comes to women. I can figure out most of the Great Spirit's creatures, but women can be…Say, are you flirting with me? Don't you see I'm old enough to be your Pa?" Eleanor reddened in embarrassment, "So what if I am? I'm a grown woman. I can do what I want!" Jake shook his head, "What would your Pa say if he could hear this conversation?" Eleanor blurted out, "Well why don't we just ask him when you come over for supper tonight?" Jake threw up his hands in disgust, "That tears it! Little girl, you need to run along back to your Pa before you get us both in trouble." Eleanor shouted after him, "My name is not "little girl." It's Eleanor…Eleanor Farnsworth!"

At Supper

That night at supper, Eleanor was still agitated as she slammed the dishes down on the table. Daniel peered over his spectacles, "Eleanor, I heard quite a tale in town today. One of my friends said you were carrying on quite an animated conversation with Jake Jackson. Care to explain?"

Eleanor sat down and began eating. Presently she looked up, "I was talking to him, but I wouldn't call it animated…It was just a discussion." Daniel responded, "A discussion?…A discussion about what?" Eleanor retorted it, "Seriously, Father, can't a girl have a little privacy?" Daniel replied, "What is private about you shouting at a strange man in public?" Eleanor softly replied, "You wouldn't understand."

Daniel continued the conversation the next morning at breakfast, "Eleanor, I don't want you to have anything to do with Jake Jackson. The man is dangerous! He has supposed to have killed countless men! Just the other day, he paraded through town half naked and dropped off three scalps at the sheriff's office. Jake Jackson is a murdering savage!"

Defiance crept in as Eleanor raised her voice, "If he's a murderer, why isn't he in jail? If Sheriff Taylor has scalps of innocent men, why hasn't he arrested Jake?" Daniel responded, "Jake Jackson is lucky he's not in jail! If we had a competent sheriff, he would be locked up!…I just don't understand. What do you see in him?" Eleanor sighed, "Father, he's like no other man I've ever met. The men I knew in Boston would feint if they had to face Jake. They were boys pretending to be men. Jake's the real thing!"

Finding Jake

The next day, Daniel sent one of the tellers from the bank to locate Jake. The teller found him at the hotel Jake was staying at. With his hat in hand, the teller asked, "Mr. Jackson, Mr. Farnsworth at the bank would like to see you at your convenience. If you would be so kind to agree, what time can I tell Mr. Farnsworth to expect you?"

Jake grimaced, "I may as well get this over with. I'll go with you back to the bank." Daniel's secretary announced, "Mr. Jackson to see you, sir." Daniel gestured to a chair in front of his desk. He didn't offer to shake hands. Daniel coolly said, "It was good of you to come, Mr. Jackson. I assume you know why I wanted to see you?" Jake nodded his head, "I suspect this is about your daughter."

Daniel had a little apprehension about speaking with Jake. He hoped he would be safe at the bank in broad daylight. Daniel exhaled, "Sir, what is your interest in my daughter, Eleanor?" Jake smiled, "I have no interest in your daughter. While I'm sure Eleanor is a fine girl, any interest has come from her. I have done my best to discourage her even pointing out the difference in our ages. Frankly, nothing seems to discourage her. I suspect she wasn't spanked enough when she was young."

In spite of himself, Daniel chuckled, "I'm afraid you've got me there, Mr. Jackson. Her mother died giving birth to Eleanor. I've never been able to deny her anything…I want her to find someone who is suitable." Jake replied, "I agree, Mr. Farnsworth. If I had a daughter, I wouldn't want her to get mixed up with the likes of someone like me." Daniel frowned, "Mr. Jackson, I'm afraid that I haven't been very fair to you. You seem like a nice enough fellow despite your reputation. I appreciate your understanding."

Blackie Davis was born an Albino with white hair, pale skin and pink eyes. Even his eyebrows were white. More than one drunk had asked him, "Feller, why are you called Blackie? I ain't seen no black on you anywheres!" Blackie always answered, "My Pa thought it would be funny to name me, Blackie. He would almost choke to death laughing." Blackie would smile, but folks didn't know what he was smiling about. He had his own laugh at the thought of his Pa's body jumping with each slug Blackie pumped into it.

Boone Helm had an aversion to work or anything that might help someone else. He had a dark secret. Boone and a friend were once stranded in the Davis Mountains. Their horses had been stolen by Apache. Leaving the two men to starve appealed to the Apache sense of humor. Once it became critical, Boone shot and killed his friend. To Boone it was only logical to dine on his friend's flesh. The ghoulish aspect of this whole sordid episode was Boone found he preferred human flesh. He liked human flank better than beef flank. Boone looked for any opportunity to kill friend or foe to add to the stew pot.

Somehow Blackie and Boone had managed to find each other to form an unholy alliance. Their partnership was made in Hell.

Blackie yelled, "Sum bitch that hurts!" The wound where the bullet creased his leg was bleeding profusely. Boone nodded, "That durn guard on that stagecoach could sure shoot that rifle! Look here, he put a hole in my hat!" Blackie responded, "Shut up, Boone! A hole in your hat don't compare to the hole in my leg!" Boone replied, "Well, I tried to tell you that robbing a stage was too much work! We need to find something where folks don't get all riled up when we take their money!" Blackie responded, "If I don't lose my leg, I have an idea how we can make some easy money."

Eleanor had received special treatment all her life. Her beauty and her father's wealth caused most folks to put her on a pedestal. Eleanor was catered to and never made to feel threatened. That made it all the more shocking when a ghostly specter grabbed her in the middle of the day and dragged her out the back door of the house. As Eleanor was being kidnapped, she saw the bashed in skull of Inez, the maid.

The Farnsworth estate was 200 wooded acres. The proximity of the trees facilitated the approach and the escape of Blackie and Boone with their victim. They rode hard for most of the day heading for the wilderness of the Davis Mountains. That night Blackie briefly ungagged Eleanor. She yelled, "Are you two completely crazy. My daddy will hire a 100 detectives by tomorrow. All of them will be looking for you! Not only that, my boyfriend is Jake Jackson. When he hears about this, I wouldn't give a plugged nickel for either one of you!...And my Jake likes taking scalps better than anything. You boys are in for a haircut!"

Blackie looked at Boone and laughed. He slapped Eleanor so hard that it knocked her down. As blood trickled from her mouth, Eleanor slowly rose to her feet. The look on her face said she wanted to say something, but she thought the better of it.

Dropping By

Jake dropped by Sheriff Taylor's office, "Sheriff, the rumor is that Eleanor Farnsworth has been kidnapped. Is that true?" Sheriff Taylor sighed, "I'm afraid it's true. The kidnappers killed their maid. The old man is in a panic. The note that was left behind said they just want $100,000. If the law tries to get involved, the note said they would kill the girl and send little pieces back to Mr. Farnsworth. He made me swear, I wouldn't interfere. Farnsworth is going to pay the money. He's just waiting on another note telling him when and where to drop the money."

Jake responded, "Sheriff, you know they'll never give that girl back regardless of how much Farnsworth pays. When they no longer have a use for her, they'll kill her!" Taylor replied, "I'm afraid you're right, Jackson, but I gave my word to Farnsworth that I wouldn't interfere. I don't know what else to do. I can't go against him."

As Jake walked to the livery stable to saddle Buck, he thought, "That girl is going to be killed if someone doesn't kill the kidnappers first." When he easily picked up their trail behind the Farnsworth house, Jake muttered, "Anyone could have found their tracks. Someone should have already been after these men." It took Jake a few days to locate their camp. They had Eleanor tied to a tree. She was dirty and bloody, but alive. Eleanor had quit commenting. Anything she said was quickly answered with a slap or a fist.

Blackie crowed, "It's gonna be good getting our hands on old man Farnsworth's money! We'll be living like kings!" Boone chuckled, "Besides, it ain't right he's got so much and we got nothing!" Boone whispered to Blackie, "If you ain't got nothing planned for the girl after we get the money, I know a way to make her body disappear. No one will find her." The insane look in Boone's eyes made Blackie's skin crawl.

Jake stepped out in the open with his right hand hovering over the butt of his Colt, "You boys might want to hold up on spending that money. I don't like your chances of even getting it." Eleanor gasped, "I knew it! I knew you'd come for me!"

Both men had been laying on their bedrolls. They jumped to their feet. Blackie demanded, "Who in thunder are you? What business is this of yours?" Boone answered, "That's Jake Jackson. I seen him in town before. Everybody acts like he's some kind of a big deal!" Blackie grinned, "Is you a big deal, Jackson? Think you can kill both of us before we kill you?" Boone added, "Hey big deal, you better ride out or you just might end up dead!"

Jake smiled as he slowly shook his head in amazement, "It's pilgrims like you boys who tickle me at your ignorance. I could handle two like you when I was riding the Wichitas at 10 years old. Unless your plan is talking me to death, pull them smoke poles. It's time to dance."

Blackie shouted, "Get him!" Eleanor got a firsthand look at why people made such a ruckus about Jake Jackson. She never saw him draw. The first thing Eleanor saw was fire belching from the end of Jake's gun. One slug hit Blackie squarely between the eyes. The bullet blasted blood and jagged pieces of skull over the ground behind the now dead outlaw. The second slug punctured Boone's chest, making mush of his heart. Jake knew that scalping them would be too traumatic for Eleanor. He satisfied his blood lust by empting his sixgun into their bodies.

When he cut Eleanor loose, she threw her arms around his neck and covered his face with kisses. When she tried to kiss him like a woman kisses a man, Jake pulled away from her. He gently said, "None of that." Eleanor exclaimed, "Honey, we can do that now! You rescued me! That shows how you really feel about me!" Jake responded, "I want you to listen to me and I mean really listen. I think of you as I would think about a daughter. I wasn't about to let these jaspers kill you, but I would have done that for any girl in that situation." Despite her claiming to listen, Eleanor still addressed Jake as Honey or Dear on the ride back to Wichita Falls.

When they entered Wichita Falls, the town became an uproar with people shouting. A few of the women rushed up to Eleanor and patted her arm, "It's so good to see you alive!" Eleanor smiled, "I wasn't worried. I knew my Jake would find me and bring me home!"

Jake figured Daniel Farnsworth would be at the bank ready to deliver the ransom wherever the kidnappers demanded. His secretary burst into his office without knocking which was a first, "Mr. Farnsworth! They got her! Eleanor's back!" Daniel exclaimed, "Who's got her?...Where is she?" Daniel bounded from behind his desk and hurried through the front door of the bank. He saw Jake Jackson leading a horse with Eleanor riding.

Eleanor slid off the horse and hurried into her father's arms. Daniel was unashamedly crying, "I was so scared I had lost you!" He addressed Jake, "Mr. Jackson, I was willing to give $100,000 to get my daughter back. The money is yours." Jake gave a wry smile, "I didn't go after Eleanor for money. I have money. I was afraid you were going to get her killed by giving in to the kidnappers' demands. You won't have to worry about those two outlaws again. They are feeding the coyotes and the buzzards. If there's ever a next time just remember, giving outlaws what they want will never satisfy them. They will always want more."

Eleanor walked over to Jake who had never gotten off Buck. She put her hand on his leg, "Honey, I'm going to make you the finest supper you've ever had. What time will you be over? I know we are both hungry." Jake glanced at Daniel before redirecting his attention to Eleanor, "Eleanor, you will make some fine young man a good wife. I don't know why you can't get this, but there is no 'we.' Buck and I are going to spend some time hunting and fishing in the Wichitas. I grew up there. I need to get back there." Eleanor smiled, "Well, after you get done hunting, when can I expect you back?" Jake threw up his hands in exasperation, "I give up!"

Jake pointed Buck's nose north and rode away. He looked back once. Eleanor was waving enthusiastically.

Hunting

It was enjoyable to be back in his old hunting grounds. Jake shot a fat mule deer doe. That night he roasted the backstrap over a fire. Jake said, "Buck ol' boy, you don't know what you're missing by not eating some of this steak." Buck continued munching on the tall green grass. Later that night, Jake lay back on his bedroll, gazing at the stars. He told Buck, "I sure love this county, but it's not the same without my Comanche family. I know they don't have a choice but to live on the reservation…Still, it's not the same. It is sad that my brothers can no longer roam wild and free. Some say that's called progress. If that's so, they can keep the progress. I don't want any part of it. I would rather die than not be free."

Pearl Hart came from a good, God-fearing family. Her father clerked at a dry goods store. Her mother was a school teacher. When she turned 18, Pearl became restless. She had no desire to clerk or to teach. Most of all, Pearl had wearied of being under her parents' control. She wanted to have the final say in what she did or said.

Pearl had saved some money helping out at the store and the school. To her parents' horror, she bought a ticket on a stagecoach to move from her Arkansas home to Ft. Worth, Texas. Her mother asked, "Pearl, why Texas? Where will you stay? What will you do?" Pearl replied with the confidence of youth, "Oh Ma, I'll figure out something. I'll be fine." Her father never said a word, literally turning his back when she walked out the door.

When Pearl stepped off the stage in Ft. Worth, the town and the people seemed too wonderful for words. The shine soon wore off when her money started to wear off. Pearl took a job as a cook in a small café. One of the regulars was Tommy Maddux. Tommy always had a big smile for Pearl, "Miss Pearl, that was mighty good! Some lucky man is going to snatch you up one day!" Pearl winked, "Now Tommy, when are you going to stop being all talk? A girl sometimes needs some action to go with the talk." Tommy grinned, "Well, how about we go on a picnic on your day off? Is that enough action?" Pearl joked, "It might be, Tommy Maddux. We'll just have to wait and see."

The Afternoon

That Sunday afternoon, Tommy took Pearl to a private spot overlooking a small lake for their picnic. The rest of the day was filled with laughter. As the sun was setting, the charming man seduced the young girls. Pearl just knew that Tommy would ask her to marry him. Pearl sighed, "Tommy, that was wonderful. You're wonderful!"

Tommy quit coming into the café for lunch. At first Pearl was concerned that he was sick or something had happened to him. After a week she knew his intentions to her were not honorable. Pearl became bitter with his rejection. She changed from a friendly, outgoing person to one that was suspicious of everyone. One day Pearl saw Tommy walking arm-in-arm with another woman. She had never experienced the kind of pain she felt that day. The next day Pearl bought a small double-barreled Derringer. It fit perfectly in her purse.

When Pearl knocked on the front door of the house on the outskirts of town, the smile on Tommy's face disappeared, "Why Pearl! What are you doing here?...Listen, I've been meaning to come see you..." Pearl cut his statement short when she placed the barrel of her gun against his forehead. Most people misjudge the damage that the small Derringer can do, especially to one's head at close range. When Pearl pulled the trigger, Tommy's skull exploded. It splattered the half-naked girl standing behind him with blood and brain matter. Pearl stopped her screaming by firing the other barrel of the Derringer pressed against the girl's temple.

Pearl went home to clean the blood off her clothes. She stared in the mirror and spoke to Tommy, "Well am I good enough for you now? And, don't be trying to blame me. You got what you deserve. Tell that hussy I said that's what you get for stealing my man!"

After a couple of days of being surly with the customers, Pearl got fired. The final straw was her response to someone saying that Tommy and a woman had been murdered. She snorted, "Murder? It sounds more like the chickens coming home to roost to me!"

In an ironic twist in her life, Pearl became a saloon girl in a bar in the low-rent district of Ft. Worth. She didn't look as selling her body was giving in to a man. In her unhinged mind, Pearl felt that she was extracting payment from all men.

When Slim finished buttoning his pants, he said, "Pearl, you ain't the same as the other half-wits that work here. You got brains. Why ain't you doing something else where you can use your smarts?" Pearl replied, "It's funny you should mention that, Slim. I have a few ideas, but I need a couple of men to help carry them out. The kind of men who ain't fussy about doing hard things for easy money." Slim furrowed his brow, "What kind of hard things? You know I ain't too fond of work. Me or none of my pards. We fancy ourselves at playing the angles. We're always on the lookout for someone who ain't paying too close attention…if you know what I mean."

Pearl looked Slim up and down as if she was seeing him for the first time. She replied, "I don't know…maybe…You got any problems when it comes to killing if it's needed?" Slim responded, "Alright Pearl, that's enough beating around the bush. What you got in mind?" Pearl face hardened, "I'm thinking of holding up stagecoaches, maybe a few banks or robbing rich folks in general. I will be the brains. I need you and one of your friends to carry out my orders." Slim didn't look convinced, "Why would you be giving the orders? I ain't never took no orders from no woman before!"

Pearl pulled her Derringer and gave Slim a close up look at the ends of the barrels, "Here's two reasons why! If someone wants to be part of my gang, they better realize I'm ramrodding this outfit! Ain't nobody else smart enough to plan jobs that won't get everyone killed! You're durn sure not smart enough or your broke ass would be hanging around this joint. And that goes for your pard too." Slim grinned, "Aww Pearl, I was just funnin'."

Slim told Lester, "Pard, I think I may have found us a bird's nest on the ground. I'm gonna throw in with someone who will do all the thinking. I'll just do the robbing and the killing…She needs one more man. I thought you might be interested." Lester replied, "She? What in tarnation do you mean by "she"? Slim stuttered, "We...well...The one giving the orders is a "she", but she's real smart. I think we can make good money with her!" Lester was never mistaken for being the sharpest knife in the drawer. He looked bewildered for a minute before answering, "If you say it will be alright, I guess it will be. You're the smartest sum bitch I know! If it's good enough for you, I'm in!"

Pearl met with her new gang members for the first time. She explained, "Our first job is going to be robbing the mercantile down the street. One of my customers works at the bank. He says Leroy, the store owner, doesn't always bring in his deposit every day. My customer says Leroy is too lazy to make daily trips to the bank. You two are going to break in the back door of the store tomorrow night after midnight. Ransack the place until you find the money. Then hightail it out of there. Bring the money back here to my room at the bar. I'll divvy it up. I get half. You two spilt the other half." Lester whined, "Why do you get half? We're the ones doing all the work!" Pearl barked, "Because it's my plan! You wouldn't even know about it if it wasn't for me! So shut up, Lester!" Lester softly replied, "Yes ma'am."

As the men got up to leave, Pearl held up her hand, "One other thing and I want y'all to pay attention. Don't let any witnesses live! Kill all witnesses! Witnesses will get us hung! You got that?" Slim and Lester nodded their heads that they understood.

Either Slim and Lester ignored the light inside the store or they didn't see it. When Slim kicked in the back door, Leroy and his wife, Maud were startled at the intrusion.

They had been restocking the shelves in anticipation of the store opening for business in the morning. Leroy declared, "See here! We're not open for business! Come back tomorrow!"

Leroy and Maud had shocked looks on their faces as slugs from the outlaws' sixguns ended their lives. Leroy lay motionless in death as blood pooled under his body. Maud fell on top of her husband, but continued to move. Lester put a bullet in her head spraying blood on the new merchandise. He apologized for killing her, "Sorry, ma'am. Pearl says we can't leave no witnesses."

When her men entered her room, Pearl grinned in anticipation, "How much did we get?" Slim stammered, "Well…it…Things didn't go like we planned." Pearl's eyes narrowed, "How much…did…we get?" Slim exclaimed, "They was there, Pearl! You said nobody'd be there that time of night! But, a man and a woman was there! By the time we shot em, it didn't leave us much time to look for loot. I did find $20."

Lester chimed in, "Look what I brung you, Pearl. I snatched this shiny necklace right off that woman's neck! I bet it will sell for a lot of money! Did I do good?" Pearl retorted, "Lester, the woman's name is spelled out on the necklace, "Maud." Are you trying to buy us a ticket to the gallows?"

Pearl wrung her hands, "I send you two out on our first job and you bring me a measly $20 and a piece of jewelry that could get our necks stretched! Good grief! What have I gotten myself into?" Slim responded, "If it makes you feel any better, you can keep my share of the $20." Pearl said, "I wasn't planning on sharing it! Do you think I'm going to pay you making a mess of a perfectly good robbery?" Pearl decided that night that she would have to go out on the future jobs herself.

Jake left the Wichitas intending to visit the Comanche on the reservation. He still had some family there. Jake knew that Burk and Quanah would use their considerable influence to persuade the Army to let him see his people. Jake enjoyed visiting with the younger brother of Red Elk. As they smoked, Jake grimaced, "I miss the old days." Lone Wolf nodded, "Reservation living is hard on the Comanche. Not all of us are wealthy like Quanah. We cannot buy our way off the reservation like he did."

When Jake got up to leave, Lone Wolf smiled, "It was good to see White Wolf. You are a legend among the Comanche. Many songs are sung about you around the campfires."

A sister of Quanah Parker and her daughter were passengers on the stage. At first the driver and the guard were uneasy about transporting Indians. The station manager reassured them, "There ain't nothing to worry about. Them two are related to ol' Quanah Parker hisself! They paid for their tickets so they're going!"

A rifle shot interrupted the bounce of the stagecoach. One of the lead horses piled up in the harness bringing the coach to a sudden stop. The driver yelled to the guard, "Shoot!" The guard already had the shotgun to his shoulder, "Where? I don't see a blamed thing to shoot at?" A barrage of gunfire eventually felled the men.

Pearl ordered, "Throw them men down along with the strongbox!" She noticed the driver and the guard were still breathing. It gave her great satisfaction to put bullets in their skulls. Slim shouted as he peered inside the coach, "Looky what we got here!" He motioned the Indian woman and girl to get out. The woman and girl showed no emotion as they stood stoically.

Lester licked his lips, "That's some mighty fine looking women…Pearl, could we?…You know." Pearl replied, "Lester, shut up! We got a job to do. We ain't got time for that nonsense. Besides, I'm still open for business, but it will cost you!"

Pearl reloaded her Derringer and put a well-placed slug between each woman's eyes.

Jake was surprised to see the Comanche trailing him. He heeled Buck from the concealment of the mesquite, "Why are you following me, brother?" The Comanche responded, "White men have murdered two of Quanah's kin. He sent me to find you. Quanah wants justice. You and Burk are the only white eyes he trusts. Burk has gotten too old for such matters."

Jake quietly listened to Quanah, "The blood of my sister and niece cries out for justice. I am not in a position to answer. Please honor our people by bringing these murderers to justice."

Jake picked up the outlaw's trail at the ambush site. He muttered as he studied the tracks, "There's three of them. The depth of one set of hoof prints says that it is either a small man or a woman." Jake waited till dusk to follow the tracks into Ft. Worth. He didn't want to be recognized if he could avoid it.

Jake pushed through the batwing doors into the dingy saloon. It was cloudy with cigarette smoke and the floor was littered with tobacco quid. Jake leaned against the bar and ordered a beer. He wasn't the least bit squeamish. Jake had once drank muddy water from a hoof track, but the condition of the filthy glass containing the beer, made him curl a lip.

Lester exclaimed, "I'm telling you, those Indian women were some prime livestock!" Pearl snapped, "Shut up, you fool before somebody hears!" It was too late. Jake noticed the two men and a woman sitting at a table in the corner. He moved in their direction leaving his beer untouched.

Jake stood directly in front of them not saying a word. Slim was irritated, "Mister, can I help you?" Jake smiled, "Maybe...I hear y'all like Indian girls. I like them myself." Pearl interjected, "This is a private conversation, sum bitch! It don't have nothing to do with you! Move on!" Jake's face hardened, "That's where you're wrong. It does have something to do with me. The two Indian women y'all murdered were kin!"

Slim, Lester and Pearl went for their guns. Slim and Lester weren't able to move their pistols more than an inch before being blasted backwards by the force of .45 slugs striking their chests from Jake's Colt. Pearl had pulled her Derringer out of her purse. A bullet from Jake's sixgun blew off most of her skull. Jake quickly scanned the room to see if anyone else were going to deal themselves in. The barkeep and the only two patrons had scurried as far away as they could get from the gunplay. Their shock turned to horror as Jake expertly scalped the three dead bodies.

Quanah examined the scalps that Jake had just presented him. He gave a slight smile, "Thank you, White Wolf. You have brought justice and honor to our people today."

Pony

Bill "Pony" Stillwell was leaning on the bar of the Last Chance Saloon in Wichita Falls, drinking whiskey. Pony had gotten his nickname for preferring small horses to accommodate his short legs. Six boisterous soldiers burst through the batwing doors. The sergeant yelled, "Whiskey, barkeep! We want all you got!" He walked over to the bar and grabbed the bottle next to Pony's shot glass, "Hey mister, I'm sure you're done with that!" Pony retorted, "Put it back! I ain't finished with it!" The soldier smirked, "You ain't listening good, you little runt! I said you were done!" The other five put their hands on the butts of their pistols in support of their sergeant. Pony stalked out of the bar. The sergeant muttered to his men, "I didn't believe that runt would want push it." They all laughed.

Pony crept up to a side window that gave him a clear view of the soldiers sitting at a near table. Without any warning, Pony began firing his sixgun. The first bullet ear-holed the loud mouth sergeant. When the smoke cleared, four soldiers were dead. Two more were severely injured.

The Army conducted an investigation on the attack of its men, but it turned up empty. The general public was appreciative of the military's role in settling the Indian wars. What they didn't appreciate was the way some soldiers ran rough shod over civilians. There was little cooperation from the locals on the shooting. Most thought the soldiers probably got what they deserved.

Every time Pony thought of the incident with the soldiers, he smirked, "Guess I ain't too little for you boys now!" Pony quickly got back to his regular business of rustling and robbing.

Pony softly spoke to the two men at a bar in Abilene, "I'm looking for a couple of boys to help me with a few cows." Abner replied, "I ain't much good with cows." Pony responded, "I ain't looking for a top hand with cattle. I'm looking for a top hand with a gun. My cattle business demands that the previous owner takes a dirt nap on Boot Hill. We drive our new herd to west Texas. I have a connection that will buy all the cows I can bring." Jess asked, "What's the split?" Pony replied, "I get half. You two split the other half." Jess responded, "That don't seem rightly fair. We taking the same risk as you. It should be a three way split." Abner interrupted, "Shut up, Jess! The man is doing all the planning and has the buyer." Abner turned to Pony, "The split is fine with us. When do we start?"

Jess didn't know how close he came to death that night. If he had turned Pony down, Pony would have killed him. Pony couldn't have anyone walking around knowing his plans without being a member of his gang.

Most rustlers stole cattle first, worried about the owner second. Pony Stillwell reversed that order. He found Abner and Jess at the same bar in Abilene. After joining their table, Pony whispered, "We leave in the morning at dawn. Meet me at the livery." Abner asked, "How big a job is it?" Pony replied, "Decent…about 500 head." Jess wanted to know, "How we gonna move that many cows with folks chasing us?" Pony grinned, "Nobody will be chasing us. They're going to be too busy pushing up daisies." Abner responded, "I'm not following. What do you mean?" Pony smirked, "There's just one old man and two hands. We kill them first. Then we can take our own sweet time driving them cattle west."

As they stood up to leave, Jess held up one finger to ask another question, "Pony, you changed your mind yet on the split?" Pony and Abner answered in unison, "Shut up, Jess!"

It took the outlaws four hours of hard riding to get to the Easy E. Pa Pa Evans was the owner of the Easy E. Down through the years, accidents, illness and disease had wiped out Pa Pa's family. He considered his two hands, Cole and Davy, along with his cattle as his family. Pa Pa even gave names to some of the cows, "Petunia, how are you this fine morning? Elsa, you're looking a little peaked. Are you feeling alright?" Cole and Davy chuckled when they heard Pa Pa carrying on conversations with the beasts. Pa Pa warned, "One day you might need one of the cows to help you. When they don't even know their own names, you'll be sorry that you didn't take the time name them." The boys grinned even wider. They loved that old man.

Just A Typical Day

It started out as a typical day on the Easy E. That changed when an eruption of gunfire cleared the saddles of Pa Pa, Cole and Davy. Pony and his henchmen rode out from the concealment of the scrub oaks to admire their handiwork. Pony laughed, "Mighty fine shootin', boys. You done good!"

Davy was dead when he hit the ground. Pa Pa and Cole's moans said they were still alive. Pony exclaimed, "Hold on! Maybe I patted you two on the back too soon." Pony slid of the back of his horse and approached the two who were still breathing. Cole was laying on his back taking jagged breaths. Pony put a bullet in his head. Pa Pa was on his belly. Pony rolled him over with the point of his boot. Pa Pa looked defiantly at the outlaw. Pony asked, "Well, old man. You got any final words?" With his last breath, Pa Pa spit out, "Go to hell, sum bitch!" Pony grinned when he looked at Abner and Jess, "At least I didn't have to waste a bullet on the old fart!" The killers rummaged through the dead men's saddle bags for anything that might be useful for the trip to west Texas.

The proceeds from the sale of the cattle kept the outlaws in whiskey and women for three weeks. When they ran out of money, Pony stated, "I deserve to live like a king. I ain't going back to sleeping on the ground and roasting a stringy jackrabbit for supper! We need to up the stakes. We going to steal more than just a few hundred at a time...Any of you boys heard of the four-sixes Ranch?" Abner replied, "Everybody's heard of the four-sixes. Biggest ranch in Texas."

Pony thought for a minute before continuing, "I heard they got lots of cattle. We could make a good haul from them. Abner asked, "I thought we were going to stick with the small outfits where we could kill the hands and not have anybody after us. That's Burk Burnett's spread. He's got a hundred cowhands. We couldn't kill all of them. That don't sound like a good idea."

Pony smiled, "You ain't the brains of this outfit. I am. What I say goes...Course it might be different if you wanted to leave us and go your separate way." The evil look on Pony's face caused Abner to crawfish, "No, you're the boss. Whatever you say. I'm with you, Pony!" Pony responded, "Let me worry about Burk Burnett and his hands. If Burnett gets too close, I'll stick a bullet in his eye. I ain't scared of him or his boys!"

Jake Rides

Burk Burnett grinned when he saw Jake ride up. Burk said, "Jake, when are you going to quit blowing around like a tumbleweed? You got a good home here. You know I ain't got no kin. The four-sixes could be yours one day...although don't be in an all-fired hurry about it. I plan on sticking around for a few more years!"

Jake warmly shook Burk's hand. Jake smiled, "Now Burk, the way I see it, you don't own this ranch. This ranch owns you...Nope, I don't want no part of that." Over supper that night Jake asked, "Burk, if it's alright with you, I think I might like to hang around a few days. This place may be the closest thing I got to a home. The open country ain't so open anymore. People are crowding in from all over. The mountains aren't the same with the Comanche living on a reservation."

Burk sadly shook his head, "I never thought that the Comanche could be brought down like that. Once the army killed and encourage the hunters to kill the buffalo, the Comanche's days were numbered. The Comanche couldn't feed themselves without the buffalo."

Jake changed the subject, "Do you still need me to ride out your ranch to make sure the thieves aren't milking you dry?" Burk replied, "That's a good idea. We got several spots that are leaking. I need you to plug the holes."

Pony had decided to make a trial run on the most western part of the four-sixes. If everything went well, he's hire a couple more men to expand his operations. Pony looked over the small valley with several hundred head grazing peacefully. He remarked, "Looks like we're in luck. There's some cows just for the taking. Ain't even no hands around that we'd have to shoot. Let's round em up and head west."

Jake heeled Buck to stand in the middle where the cattle were moving. Pony was surprised and jerked the reins of his horse at the sight of the lone rider. The outlaw demanded, "Move, mister or we'll move you. And I can promise you if we have to move you, you won't like it!" Jake grinned, "I ain't too worried about a half-pint like you moving me." Jake then addressed his horse, "What about you, Buck? You worried?" Buck tossed his head. Jake spoke to Pony again, "See there, ol' Buck ain't worried neither."

Abner and Jess had joined Pony. All three horses stood side by side. Pony asked, "What's your name, stranger. Somebody might want to put a marker on your grave," Jake's eyes narrowed, "The name is Jake Jackson." Jess exclaimed, "Hey, I heard of you! Ain't you supposed to be some kind of a fancy gunfighter? Can you show me some gun tricks?" Again Pony and Abner shouted in unison, "Shut up, Jess!"

While still mounted, Pony jerked Jess off his horse using his body as a shield. Pony drew his pistol and began firing at Jake. Jake's first two bullets erased the bewildered look from Jess's face. Jess was dead, but his body was still an effective shield. Jake's third bullet thumped into the chest of Abner. Abner had been in the process of pulling his sixgun when the slug from Jake's Colt knocked him to the ground. A lucky shot from Pony penetrated Jake's left arm.

Pony was overjoyed to see the dust fly from the impact of his bullet on Jake's shirt. It didn't take long until that sleeve was red with blood. Pony crowed as he hid behind Jess's body, "Hey Jackson, how'd you like that shot? Maybe you ain't as good with a gun as folks say?" His next shot burned the front shoulder of Buck. The horse was a veteran of many gun battles. Buck flinched at the burn of the bullet, but held his ground.

Pony figured he was winning and got overconfident. He accidently exposed too much of his head. Jake shot off one of Pony's ears. The pain of losing an ear caused Pony to drop Jess. Jake quickly followed up with a bullet through Pony's heart. Unexpectedly, Jake emptied his gun into Pony's body.

When Jake threw three scalps at the feet of Burk who was sitting on his front porch, he stated, "I plugged a hole over on your west pasture today." A shocked Burk replied, "Great job, son…but…but, did you have to scalp em? Times are changing. Folks just aren't as tolerant of taking your enemies' hair as they used to be." Burk coughed before continuing, "Nowadays, some people would call it uncivilized. Why did you feel the need to scalp em?"

Jake never changed the calm expression on his face, "They shot my horse."

A Proposal

Ruger Schmidt was raised in wealth and privilege in eastern Germany. His father owned a considerable amount of stock in Mauser, the arms company. That connection got young Ruger a prototype of the new bolt action rifle with telescopic sights. Ruger yearned for a more adventurous lifestyle. At first he thrilled to hunting stag. That thrill lost its appeal when he was offered a job as a man hunter.

Baron von Giger wielded power and influence in Germany. There was a persistent rumor that insisted his power was even greater behind the scene. The Baron approached Ruger discretely, "I could use a young man like you. I have heard of your prowess with your rifle. Hunting deer is one thing. Hunting a man is something much more thrilling."

Ruger was taken aback initially at the Baron's proposal. The more he thought about it, the more it intrigued him. He sent a message to the Baron. The message said simply, "Proposal accepted."

There were many strong willed men in Germany. Some found themselves on opposite sides of von Giger's business interests. Their opposition was eliminated by a well-placed bullet from long range. Ruger was fascinated as well as excited by living the life of an assassin for hire.

That came crashing down when the Baron summoned Ruger to his estate. Von Giger informed him, "Schmidt, I called you here today to inform you that your services are no longer needed. I have made other arrangements." The Baron turned on his heels and marched out of the room. Ruger was bewildered. He thought, "What have I done? Why would von Giger make this change? I didn't do this job for money. I have money…I just don't get it."

Despite being wealthy, the Baron made the change over simple economics. He found someone who would be cheaper. It was the kind of thinking that led von Giger to kill innocent men over money matters. The Baron would never have enough money.

The next morning Ruger was brooding as he walked through his garden. The bark exploded on a tree next to his head. As Ruger ran back to the shelter of his home, bullets kicked up dirt at his heels. He gasped for breath safely inside the house. The question mark in his head cleared up.

Ruger muttered, "von Giger." The Baron wanted no loose ends. Ruger realized he was now a loose end.

Two days later, von Giger was counting money in his favorite room of the house. It had a large window giving him a view of his palatial estate. The bullet from the Mouser crashed through the glass pane. It split the Baron's skull open, splashing red blood and gray brain matter all over the newly counted money.

Ruger knew he had no time to waste. His bags were packed in the buggy that was waiting for him. Ruger quickly stashed the rifle in its case and drove the buggy to the docks. Ruger had already purchased a ticket on a ship that was leaving for America that morning. He didn't say goodbye to family members or friends. Ruger never saw any of them again.

When the ship docked in New York, his first trip was to a bank to exchange German Thalers for U.S. dollars. After greasing a few palms, Ruger bought a phony set of identification papers on the black market identifying himself as Andrew Hall. He booked passage on a series of trains that landed him in Kansas City.

Ruger realized that his sudden disappearance coupled with the assassination of Baron von Giger would point the finger at himself as the killer. The fact that von Giger's tentacles reached to America, made a new identity a necessity. The Baron's family would search for the assassin regardless of where he went. As Andrew Hall, Ruger would explain his German accent due to being raised by his mother of German descent.

The new Andrew Hall set himself up in the plushest hotel in Kansas City. The leading men and women of the city immediately began to wonder about the wealthy stranger. Andrew met and was befriended by Eric Decker. Decker was the president of the largest bank in Kansas City. He hoped Andrew would select his bank as a depository for his money.

Decker smiled, "I say Andrew, old boy, you must join our men's club. Its membership is by invitation only. Of course, I will be happy to sponsor you. Lots of good business contacts there if you're so inclined. Frankly, the club gives us a chance to drink a little whiskey, smoke the best Cuban cigars and play a little cards. The best part?...No women allowed especially wives!" Decker slapped his knee as he laughed uproariously.

The most interesting man Andrew met at the club was Jack Wilson. Wilson was a rich cattleman who owned ranches in Kansas, Oklahoma and Texas. As they were visiting over whiskey and cigars, Jack asked Andrew, "So, Mr. Hall, if you don't mind me asking, are you a businessman?" Andrew paused before he answered, "I am sort of a businessman. I settle disputes between businessmen."

Recently, the desire to hunt and kill men flared up in Andrew's soul. He tried to find other interests to take the place of being an assassin. Nothing had the flavor of killing an unsuspecting man at long distance. There was nothing as thrilling as watching a bullet destroy someone's head or heart.

Jack Wilson continued, "Exactly how do you settle these disputes? Are you a trained negotiator?" Andrew gave a wry smile, "Let's just say I have a skill that most men do not have. When I settle something, the outcome is final."

Wilson pondered on what Andrew had said. A week later, he pulled Andrew over to a quiet corner in the club. Wilson stated, "Mr. Hall, I've been thinking about what you told me the other day. I have a situation that is a problem to me. I'm interested in seeing how you would solve it. I have tried to buy the largest ranch in Texas to add to my other holdings. The man who owns it won't even talk to me about selling it. He's an older man who should be more concerned about how close to move his rocking chair to the fire instead of running a big cattle operation." Andrew was nodding his head as he was listening to the rancher.

Wilson took a drag on his cigar. When he exhaled, he watched the blue smoke rise to join the cloud hovering over the room. Wilson asked, "So, Mr. Hall, how would you solve my dilemma?" Andrew stroked his chin, "First, I need to know how much you really want that ranch? Is there something you wouldn't do to get it? Second, you need to know that my skills don't come cheap. I also guarantee my work. If I don't solve your problem, you don't pay me."

Wilson replied, "There isn't anything I wouldn't do to get this ranch. The four-sixes would be the crown jewel of my holdings…You've got my attention, Mr. Hall. What do you charge?" Andrew laughed, "Mr. Wilson, I can assure you if you have to ask, you can't afford me! After getting the particulars, I will give you a price. You pay half up front. The balance is due when the job is finished."

After getting all the details from Wilson, Andrew gave him a price. Wilson stated, "Meet me at Decker's bank in the morning. I will pay you the first half. When the transaction was completed, Wilson thought, "It's your own fault, Burk Burnett that it's come to this. I was willing to pay you top dollar for the four-sixes, but you ignored me. You're going to find out that I'm not a man to ignore."

Burk was content to doze in his rocking chair on the front porch. He liked to dream of the good old days of his youth. Burk was pleased with the current condition of his ranch. The future never looked brighter.

The bullet hit before the sound did. Burk slumped in his chair as blood pooled underneath it. The ranch foreman, Clyde Fincher happened to be back at headquarters getting a change of horses. His horse had picked up a stone that wedged under its shoe resulting in it becoming lame.

Clyde rushed to Burk and began barking orders, "Toby, come help me get Burk inside. Ed, you ride hell-bent-for-leather and fetch Doc. There's no time to waste. Every second counts!" As Clyde helped carry Burk, he glanced nervously around scanning the horizon. He knew the shooter was still out there somewhere probably watching them.

Jake Returns

When Jake got in that afternoon from checking on cattle in several pastures, he was surprised to see Doc's buggy tied up in front of the house. Clyde and several hands were talking on the porch. When Clyde saw Jake, he stepped towards him, "It's Burk. He's been shot. Doc ain't sure he's gonna make it."

Jake asked, "Who shot him?" Clyde shrugged, "We don't know. I was here when it happened. I couldn't see nobody. Funny thing is I heard the thud of the bullet way before I heard the sound of the shot. I reckon the shooter must have been a ways off. I have no idea which direction."

Jake went inside to check on Burk. Burk looked like he was at death's door. Jake looked at the doctor, "Doc?" Doc sighed, "I don't know. He's in pretty bad shape. I've done all I can do, but that may not be enough." Jake stepped back outside, "Clyde, I'm going to go see if I can pick up the trail of the shooter…He doesn't know it, but there's no place on earth where he can hide from me. Burk has been a father to me."

Jake almost gave up looking. He rode wider and wider circles searching for tracks. Jake found nothing. He thought to himself, "There's got to be something I'm overlooking. This sum bitch didn't just drop down from the sky." On a hunch, Jake kept widening his circles. Finally, he found the killer's tracks. He looked back at the house and whistled, "That's got to be 700 yards! What kind of gun can shoot that far?...That makes no sense!"

Jake mounted and told Buck, "I don't know how long this will take, but we ain't stopping until we find out who shot Burk!" Jake trailed the shooter all the way to Ft. Worth to a livery stable. He asked the man in charge as he pointed at a particular horse, "Who owns that animal?" The man replied, "We do. That's one of our rentals. The feller who rented him just got back a few hours ago." Jake demanded, "What's his name?" The man responded, "I don't guess I rightly know. He had him for almost a week, but I don't recall him giving me a name. I was reluctant to rent my horse out for that long, so the man bought him. When he returned, he said I could have the horse back for free…My lucky day, huh?"

Frustration set in as Jake asked, "Can you tell me anything about that jasper?...anything at all? He shot a good friend of mine!" The man backed up a couple of steps, "Now hold on, Mister. I don't want to get involved in something that ain't none of my business." Jake grabbed the man by the front of his shirt and pulled him close, "You're already involved! If I find out you know something and didn't tell me, you're going to see the Comanche come out in me!" The man sputtered, "I..I don't know much. He took off in the direction of the train station…One other thing, he carried what looked like a rifle case." Jake turned the man loose and smoothed out his shirt, "Thanks, pard. I appreciate it."

Jake headed back to the four-sixes. He knew that going to the train station was a waste of time with no description and no destination. Maybe he could find something back at the ranch to give him a clue to the shooter's identity.

Clyde had a quizzical look on his face when Jake rode up, "Find anything?" Jake replied, "I trailed him to Ft. Worth. I think he caught a train, but I don't know where…I don't even know what he looks like. How's Burke doing?" Clyde grinned, "That old coyote is tougher than a new boot.

He's still a long way from being able to get out and around, but I think he's going to make it!"

Jake sat by the edge of the bed until Burk opened his eyes. The old man whispered, "It's good to see you, son. Clyde told me you went after the feller who shot me. I don't see no scalp so I reckon you didn't find him." Jake smiled, "Not yet, Burk but I will. Have you had a problem with anybody lately?" Burk responded, "No, nobody I can think of…Wait a minute, there was that polecat who wanted to buy the four-sixes. I didn't like the looks of him so I told Clyde to run him off. He claimed he was some kind of big shot who owned a bunch of ranches. Didn't make no difference to me what he owned, I won't ever sell the four-sixes." Jake continued, "Did the man give a name or say where he was from?" Burk replied, "I think he said his name was Jack…Jack…Jack something or other. Wait, it was Jack Wilson. He made a big deal about coming all the way from Kansas City to see me…Hell, I didn't tell the sum bitch to come down here. That's on him."

Jake checked in with Fred, the barkeep at the Longhorn Saloon in Ft. Worth, "Fred, you ever hear of a big rancher named Jack Wilson? I think he may be from Kansas City." Fred scratched his head, "Now that you mention it, there is a Jack Wilson who owns some ranches down in south Texas. I don't know if he's from Kansas City or not." After making the long ride to Presidio, Jake asked the sheriff, "You know a man named Jack Wilson?" The Sheriff replied, "There's a man by the name of Jack Wilson who owns a couple of big spreads down here. I ain't never laid eyes on him. He's one of those that they call, an absentee owner. One of the ramrods told me Wilson lived in Kansas City."

When Jake got back to Ft. Worth, he wasn't sure about what to do with Buck. The big stud didn't cotton to any man except for Jake. If anybody else tried to touch him, Buck would do his best to kick their head off. In the end, Jake booked passage on a train bound for Kansas City for both of them. Jake decided to ride in the stock car to make sure Buck got fed and nobody got killed.

After the train arrived in Kansas City, Jake boarded Buck at a livery stable with strict orders for no one to touch him. Jake said he would be back to feed Buck. He asked for directions to the biggest bank in Kansas City. Jake figured that if this Wilson was a big shot, a banker would know about him.

Jake read that Eric Decker was the president of the bank on its sign out front. Jake requested from the lady sitting at the first desk he came to, "I need to see Mr. Decker." She replied, "Is Mr. Decker expecting you." Jake wasn't dressed like their normal banking customer. She was also a little alarmed at the Colt on his hip. Jake answered, "Tell Mr. Decker that Jake Jackson is here to see him." The look on Jake's face caused the secretary to retreat to the back offices.

In a few minutes a man emerged from one of the offices. He cautiously approached Jake, "Mr. Jackson? Jake Jackson?" Jake nodded, "I'm Jake Jackson." The man continued, "THE Jake Jackson? The famous gunfighter?" Jake just stared at him. The man stuck his hand out, "I don't believe this. Jake Jackson, here in my bank!...You're not going to rob us, are you?" Jake joked, "It's been weeks since I robbed a bank." It took Decker a minute to realize that Jake wasn't serious. He laughed as he shook Jake's hand, "Sorry, Mr. Jackson. We don't get someone who is famous in our bank every day. Please excuse me!...Tell me, sir, how can I help you?" Jake motioned towards the back, "Have you got someplace where we can talk in private?'

Decker took a seat behind his huge desk while Jake sat in one of the chairs facing him. Decker raised his eyebrows in anticipation of a question. Jake said, "I represent a party who owns the largest ranch in Texas. I am looking for a qualified buyer. One of the bankers in Ft. Worth recommended that I start with you. He felt that you might know someone with enough money who could have an interest in buying the property." Decker responded, "That's easy! You want to talk to Jack Wilson. That sounds like something he would be interested in. I can take you over to his office if you'd like." Jake shook his head, "That won't be necessary. All I need is the address."

Jake didn't bother to knock on the front office door for Jack Wilson. He let myself in and immediately started for the door of the back office. Wilson's secretary jumped up protesting, "Sir! Sir! You can't go back there!" She tried to block Jake's path, but Jake brushed her aside. A startled Jack Wilson exclaimed, "Mister, I don't know who you are, but you better have a damn good reason to barge in my office like this! I'll have the Sheriff put you in jail!" Jake grinned, "Go ahead. Call him. He might be interested in the shooting of a respected cattleman down in Texas. And how the trail of the killer led to you." Wilson paused then spoke to his secretary, "It's okay, Doris. Please close the door on your way out."

He turned to Jake, "Now what in blue blazes are you talking about? I don't know anything about any killing in Texas. How do you figure I was involved in it?" Jake sat down in one of the over-stuffed leather chairs. His eyes narrowed when he spoke, "I'm a good friend of Burk Burnett. I know you tried to buy his ranch and he threw you off the four-sixes. Burk was shot the other day. I think you hired the shooter to kill Burk to steal his ranch at auction. By the way, you might be interested in knowing that when I left Texas, Burk was alive and kicking."

Wilson flinched at the news that Burk was alive. He demanded, "Who the devil are you?" Jake replied, "Jake Jackson." Wilson responded, "The gunfighter?" Jake shrugged, "I know how to use a gun." Wilson sputtered, "You made the trip from Texas for nothing. I don't know who shot Mr. Burnett, but it had nothing to do with me. Now if you'll excuse me, I have work to do." Jake smiled, "Have it your way for now. I'm going to see to it that you pay for what you done."

Jake watched from the concealment of a dark alley across from the bank. He chuckled as he had figured right. Wilson came out of the building where his office was located. He entered the Baltimore Hotel, just down the street. Jake trailed Wilson watching him go up the stairs in the hotel. Jake asked the clerk at the front desk, "I just saw Jack Wilson go up the stairs. He's an old friend of mine. I wanted to say, howdy. Which room did he go to?" The clerk smiled, "I'm sorry, sir. We're not allowed to give out that kind of information." Jake jerked out his knife and pressed the blade to the clerk's throat, "Tell me the room number and the name of the man who's is staying there or I'm going to start slicing at your throat and end up at your scalp!"

The clerk urinated in his pants as blood began to trickle down his neck, "It's room 206. That's Mr. Andrew Hall's room." Jake returned his knife to its sheaf, "Let's keep this little conversation between you and me. Otherwise I might be forced to come back and pay you another visit."

Wilson knocked on 206. Andrew said, "Come in." Andrew could see that Wilson was in a rage, "Jack, what's the problem?" Wilson said in hushed tones, "The problem is you lied to me. The problem is you took money from me under false pretenses. The problem is you botched the job. The problem is Burk Burnett isn't dead. The problem is Burk Burnett is very much alive."

Andrew's brow furrowed, "That can't be. I shot him. I watched him die." Wilson retorted, "You are a liar and a thief." Andrew responded, "Watch yourself, Wilson. There's a line you shouldn't cross. You're right up against it. If the man's still alive, I will refund your money. Who told you that Burnett was still alive?" Wilson began to calm down, "I got a visit today from a friend of Burnett, a gunfighter by the name of Jake Jackson. He threatened me…You need to do something." Andrew paced the floor for a minute, "Find out where this Jackson is staying. I will take care of it."

That night Wilson woke up with a strange prickling sensation on the back of his neck. The shadow in his bedroom suddenly moved. The butt of Jake's Colt dented Wilson's skull sending him back to sleep. Wilson's wife asleep in an adjoining bed never stirred.

Jake had located a densely wooded area in a river bottom not far from Kansas City. When Wilson regained consciousness, he was staked out, spread-eagled on the ground. The cool breeze raised goosebumps on Wilson's naked flesh.

Wilson's vision finally focused. He could see a small fire with the blade of a large knife being heated in the flames. Jake was squatted, staring intensely at Wilson. The fear induced bile rose from Wilson's stomach to sour his mouth, "Jackson, what do you want? Do you want money? I can make you rich!" Jake shook his head, "I don't want your money. I have money. I want justice for my friend, Burk Burnett." Wilson protested, "If you want justice, this isn't the way to get it. Take me into town and have the Sheriff arrest me. Make me stand trial. That's the way to get justice!"

Jake snorted, "That's white man's justice. I'm not interested in that. Your money could buy your way out of that justice. The justice you'll get is Comanche justice. I will peel the skin bit by bit from your body. I will cauterize the wounds keeping you from bleeding to death too fast. I can make it last several days. You will pay for what you did to Burk."

Jack Wilson began to scream before the edge of the knife ever touched his skin.

Rumours, and more Rumours

The latest rumor at the men's club was that Jack Wilson was missing. So far a large man hunt had turned up nothing. Fear settled in Andrew's stomach like a large stone sinking into the bottom of a well. Andrew hurried back to the hotel to pack his bags. He intended to catch the next train out of town regardless of its destination.

When Andrew entered his hotel room, he was shocked to feel the barrel of a gun pressed to his temple. Jake commanded in a whisper, "Don't say anything. Your next word will be your last." Jake tied him up and crammed a gag in his mouth. Jake warned, "Be still if you don't want to feel a bullet split your head open like a ripe melon." Andrew didn't realize that it would have been better to elect to take the bullet in the head over what was in store for him. Later that night, a blow to the head from Jake rendered Andrew unconscious. Jake trundled Andrew to that same location on the river bottom.

When Andrew came to, he was met by two horrors. One was the realization that he was staked out naked. The second was that next to him in the same position was the rotting corpse of his former business partner, Jack Wilson. Andrew began to cry when he saw that Wilson's body looked like a skinned squirrel. He begged, "Please, I'm not really Andrew Hall. My real name is Ruger Schmidt. My family is extremely wealthy. I can make you rich beyond your wildest dreams!"

Jake raised an eyebrow, "This must be my lucky week. That's the second offer I've had to make me rich." Andrew began to scream when Jake turned the knife in the fire to make sure it heated evenly. It was a number of years before a deer hunter found the grisly remains.

Eric Decker wondered in light of the disappearance of Jack Wilson and Andrew Hall if he should tell the Sheriff about the visit from Jake Jackson. In the end he decided against it. Decker didn't want to take the chance of offending Jake. He figured Jake would appreciate him leaving the name of Jake Jackson out of it. An offended Jake Jackson was the last person Decker wanted to see.

Jake had his fill of train rides. He took the much longer option of riding back to Texas. Jake figured Buck would agree too. After buying provisions, Jake pointed Buck's nose south. Several weeks later, Jake was overjoyed to see Burk sitting in his rocker on the front porch when he rode up. It was hard to say who had the biggest grin, Burk or Jake. As Jake tossed the two scalps on the porch, he said, "These two ol' boys won't be bothering you anymore." Burk was so glad to see Jake that he didn't even scold him for scalping the two men.

Hathaway

Anne Hathaway had been widowed for more than two years. Initially she wondered if she would ever recover from the unexpected death of her beloved husband, Bob. He had been thrown by an unruly horse. The fall had broken his neck. Bob had been the only man she had ever loved. Gradually time began to soften her pain. Anne sold their ranch and bought a small house in Wichita Falls.

One day she was strolling down a wooden sidewalk admiring the dresses and other items being displayed in shop windows. She twirled a parasol that was protecting her pretty face from the fierce Texas sun. Anne suddenly stopped at the approach of a cowboy. There were many cowboys in Wichita Falls. There was something different about this particular cowboy. His presence commanded respect.

Jake tipped his hat as he passed the beautiful woman. He barely noticed women since his wife, Macy had been killed. But something about this woman caught his attention. When Anne "accidently" dropped her purse, Jake quickly retrieved it. He handed her the purse and stated the obvious, "You dropped this, ma'am." Anne smiled, "Who said chivalry is dead? Thank you, Mr..Mr.." Jake tipped his hat again, "Jake Jackson, ma'am." Anne replied, "Thank you, Mr. Jackson. Finally a man with manners." Both continued on their way, each wondering about the other.

Jake was a master at focusing on the task at hand. After the chance meeting with the beautiful woman, her image kept creeping into his mind. Jake was disgusted with himself that he hadn't gotten her name. He made a special trip into town from the four-sixes to see if he couldn't discover who the woman was. Jake stepped into the dress shop where he had seen the mystery woman browse the dresses from outside. The lady clerk asked, "Can I help you, sir? Is there a particular dress I can show you?"

An embarrassed Jake stuttered, "No… No, I'm not interested in a dress. I met a woman the other day as she was passing your shop. I was curious if you might know her?" After he described her, the clerk said, "That could only be Miss Hathaway. Miss Hathaway is very noticeable."

After an awkward silence, the clerk laughed, "I take it you're interested in information about Miss Hathaway? I can tell you that she's a widow. Don't get your hopes up, she's turned down every eligible bachelor in town." Jake denied, "No! No, that's not it…" Jake turned on his heels and quickly exited the store. He could hear the clerk continue to laugh as he was leaving.

After locating Anne's house, Jake walked up the path to knock on the front door. He wondered, "Why am I so blasted nervous? I've faced hostile Indians and renegade outlaws without sweating like this. This is loco."

Anne was delighted to see Jake with his hat in his hand when she opened the door. She didn't want to reveal her growing feelings toward him just yet. Anne hoped he couldn't hear her blood pounding through her veins. Maintaining her composure, she stated, "Mr. Jackson. I'm surprised to see you here. Is there something you needed?" For a split second Jake was tempted to tell Anne exactly what he needed. Instead he said, "You were just so nice the other day, I wondered if you would consider joining me for a picnic this Sunday afternoon?"

Anne pretended to think it over before saying, "Mr. Jackson, that sounds just lovely. Don't worry about the food. I'll prepare everything. What time will you come by to pick me up?" Jake replied, "Will two o'clock be alright?" Anne laughed, "That will be fine, but on one condition…You call me Anne. I call you Jake." Jake grinned, "That's the best idea I've heard in a long time…Anne." Anne responded, "Then it all settled. I'll see you Sunday afternoon…Jake."

Jake couldn't remember the last time he was as happy as he was on that Sunday afternoon. Jake parked the buggy under a grove of cottonwoods overlooking a small lake. He and Anne talked for hours. Anne's fried chicken was the best he'd ever eaten. As the sun started to set, Jake drove the buggy by the house to introduce Anne to Burk. Burk clasped Anne's hand warmly with both of his, "Anne, it's a pleasure to meet you." Anne smiled broadly, "Mr. Burnett, it's my pleasure. The four-sixes is a beautiful place." Burk responded, "It's never been more beautiful than with your presence today." Jake interjected, "Ease up, old man. I saw her first." When the laughter died down, Anne joked, "Jake Jackson, you hush up now. Mr. Burnett knows how to treat a lady."

Jake, Anne and Burk sat in the parlor. They visited for another hour. When Jake and Anne were leaving, Burk said, "Honey if this jasper gives you any problems, you just let ol' Burk know. I'll take a tomahawk to him!" Jake added, "The bad thing is, he's not kidding!"

When Jake and Anne were saying good night at her front door, Anne remarked, "I loved meeting Burk. I can see why you think so much of him." Impulsively Jake leaned in for a kiss. Anne pulled back slightly as she gently put her hand on his face. She promised, "Not yet...but soon."

The next day Burk said to Jake, "I sure liked Miss Anne. She's all class. You better get your brand on her before some cowboy with better sense than you snaps her up!" Jake replied, "This is the first time I've had those kind of feelings for a woman since Macy died." Burk softened, "I know, son. Macy's death hit me hard too, her and y'all's baby. Losing both of them is something that no one should have to go through. We know that living on the frontier is a hard life. Hard things happen. Knowing Macy like I did, she would want you to move on and be happy. I sorta feel like Macy would approve of Anne." Jake nodded, "I never thought of it that way, but I agree. I think she would approve of Anne. Anne reminds me some of Macy."

Elwood Tinker had been a bully since he figured out he was naturally bigger and stronger than the other children his age. His father never set an example for him as he deserted his mother, Molly before he was born. Molly crawled into a bottle to try to escape the hopelessness of trying to raise a child with no job. She knew she had one talent, but decent folk frowned on using that talent for financial gain.

Molly began to advertise that she would take in dirty clothes for washing. It was odd that she denied any requests made by women. She only accepted business from men. A male customer complained, "Hey, these clothes are exactly like I brung em. You ain't done a durn thing to them!" Molly replied, "Do I look like the kind of girl who would wash your dirty socks?" The bewildered customer asked, "Well if you ain't the kind of girl who washes socks, what kind of girl are you?" Molly slipped off her blouse as an answer.

Men beat a steady path to her door. The women in her neighborhood in Weatherford despised Molly. The men didn't seem to mind. The problem was Molly spent as much as she made on liquor. She was always drunk and Elwood was always ignored. Some of the men noticed and started bringing groceries to feed Elwood. Elwood wasn't very old before he figured out what was going on behind the paper-thin walls of his momma's bedroom.

Molly died the summer Elwood turned 12. Her destroyed liver finally quit. Since he was the size of a grown man, no one was concerned about Elwood's welfare. The old shack became the home of a couple out-of-control teenagers who Elwood met on the streets. His small gang had a roof over their heads, but they still need food to eat.

Jumper Jim complained, "We gotta get organized. We got us some good men, but we ain't using them right. We need someone who knows the best way to rustle horses and cows. We need someone who is good at planning robberies and stick ups. Otherwise we're going to keep scraping by with barely enough to eat. And that ain't good when you got Hog around!" The overweight Hog snorted, "Hey, I got big bones. They need food." Jumper Jim retorted, "It ain't about your bones! It's about your fat belly. That's what you keep feeding?" Hog shrugged, "Maybe."

Elwood asked Jumper Jim, "How'd you get the name, Jumper?" Jumper Jim laughed, "When I was a tadpole, my old man was trying to whoop me with a razor strap. He was always yelling, 'Quit that dang jumping around, Jim. You're wearing me out!' I've been called Jumper Jim for as long as I can remember."

On the surface the three boys seemed to be just ordinary teenagers. They weren't. The glue that held them together was they shared a mean streak. Not just mischievous but down-right evil mean.

The elderly lady pleaded, "Y'all take whatever you want, just don't hurt me!" Elwood snickered, "Why we wouldn't do that, would we Jump?" Jumper Jim grinned, "Of course not. We ain't like that atall! Cept Hog might eat her if he's hungry enough!" Hog grunted that he might.

Elwood had enough when he spoke to their victim, "Lady, we're three hungry boys. You got no grub except a little bread. At your age you should have money or jewelry or something we could sell for money. You got nothing. You ain't no use to no one!"

Elwood took the butcher's knife from the kitchen and slashed the old woman's throat. He was fascinated that there could be that much blood in a human body. Jumper Jim asked, "Why'd you do that?" Elwood replied, "Cause I knowed you and Hog have already killed some folks. How do you think that makes me feel? I'm just as good as y'all. I want to be a part. Besides I ain't never seen no one die before. I figured now was a good time to start." Hog grunted his approval.

Later Elwood remarked, "Boys, it ain't right we got no guns! Hell, we only got one knife between us. And that the one I stole from that old woman. How are people going to respect us if they ain't scared we might blast em. We need us some shootin' irons!"

That night the young outlaws broke into the mercantile. They carried off a number of guns and some tools they could sell cheap for some cash.

Homer Newsome, the owner of the mercantile, yelled at the lawman, "Sheriff, they almost cleaned me out! I may have to close the store. I ain't sure I can afford to stay in business. What are you going to do about this?" Sheriff Barker sighed, "We're working on it, Mr. Newsome. Me and my deputies will find the thieves. You just gotta give us a little time." Homer continued to shout, "I ain't got no time! I need my merchandise back now!" Sheriff Barker didn't respond.

When the Sheriff tried to reason out who might have robbed the mercantile, he kept thinking about the three hoodlums who lived in the shack at the edge of town. At first it didn't make any sense. Those boys were a nuisance with petty theft, but it's a pretty big stretch to connect them to robbing the mercantile and to the cold-blooded murder of the elderly woman. Since he didn't have any other suspects, Sheriff Barker decided to pay them a visit.

The knock at the front seemed especially loud. It startled Jumper Jim and Hog who were in what passed as a living room. Before they could respond. Sheriff Barker kicked in the door. He and his deputy entered the old shack with guns drawn. The Sheriff declared after a quick scan of the room, "Well, what do we have here? Where'd you boys get all them guns? I guess I'd be wasting my breath to ask for a bill of sale!"

Elwood was in the back room practicing his draw in front of the cracked mirror. When he heard the Sheriff shouting, he cocked his pistol and slowly edged his way toward the front. Sheriff Barker ordered, "You two get away from them guns. March over here and turn around so my deputy can cuff you…Where is your other running buddy? Where's he at?"

Elwood said right before he pulled the trigger, "Right here, Sheriff." The slug from Elwood's shot entered the back of the lawman's neck. Its exit scattered blood and a jagged edge of his spine all over Jumper Jim and Hog. In his haste to shoot his gun, the deputy fumbled it. His pistol ended up on the floor. The terrified deputy threw up his hands, "I give up! Don't shoot!" Elwood smirked, "Sorry, you got to go." The next shot punched a hole in the deputy's heart. A brief vision of his wife and young daughter flashed through his mind before he died.

Jumper Jim was in a panic as he frantically wiped off the blood, "We got to hurry and get out of here. Somebody must have heard the shots. It won't be long before they come for a look…Hog, wipe off that blood you dumb sum bitch! We don't want anyone to be wondering why you got blood all over you!"

They quickly loaded as many of the guns as they could in the lawmen's saddle bags. Both men had carbines in a scabbard on their saddles. Elwood strapped on the Sheriff's pistol and holster. Jumper Jim did the same with the deputy's. They helped hoisting Hog onto the biggest horse. The horse staggered a bit adjusting to Hog's weight. Jumper Jim and Elwood rode double on the other horse.

A Meeting

Ten miles down the road leading west out of Weatherford, they met a cowboy coming to town. The cowboy chuckled at Hog, "Hey ol' son, is your horse going to make it? It looks like you might have had one to many helpings of biscuits and gravy." Without any warning,

Elwood shot the jovial cowboy. Jumper Jim slid off from behind Elwood and mounted the dead cowboy's horse. A sense of power came over Elwood as they rode along. They had horses and guns. His gang was going places! Elwood promised himself, "Someday everyone would know the name, Elwood Tinker! I am going to be somebody!" Elwood confused his two partners when he laughed out loud.

The first time Elwood referred to their group as the Tinker Gang, it brought a sharp rebuke from Jumper Jim, "Wait! What? How come we're the Tinker Gang? Why ain't we the Jumper Jim Gang or the Hog Gang? Why do you get to name the gang?" Hog was moved to speak. He grunted, "I like the sound of the Hog Gang. It will make folks think we're first class!" Elwood rolled his eyes, "You boys are loco. The Jumper Jim Gang makes us sound like we're a bunch of damn frogs! The only thing worse than that is the Hog Gang. I don't like rolling in the mud!"

Elwood paused, "I say we're gonna be the Tinker Gang. Anybody that says different can pull on me!" Elwood put his hand on his gun butt. Jumper Jim briefly considered it, but ultimately decided it wasn't worth gun play. The Hog Gang idea quickly left Hog's mind. He never thought about it again.

Jake leaned up against the bar in the Last Chance Saloon in Wichita Falls sipping a beer. He couldn't help but notice the three cowboys seated at a table in the corner. They were drunk and a little loud. The cowboys were also peculiar looking too. One was arrogant, spouting off like he was an expert on everything. One was jumpy, always jerking his head like someone might be sneaking up on him. The third was as fat as a corn-fed steer about to go to market. He made an odd snorting noise when he talked.

Elwood announced to the entire bar, "I was beginning to think Wichita Falls have the ugliest women in Texas. I changed my mind when I come across a fine a piece of female flesh as I ever seen! Some ol' boy told me her name was Anne. Next time I see her, I'm gonna bulldog her on the spot and show her what a real man is like!" Jumper Jim and Hog joined Elwood in raucous laughter.

It took Jake two steps to cross the floor to their table. His first punch hit Elwood flush on the point of his chin. The power of the blow lifted Elwood off his feet leaving him slumped against the wall, out cold. Jake mule kicked Hog, breaking his nose and sending him sprawling on the floor in his own blood. Jumper Jim was doing his best to get away, but Jake was too fast for him. Jake hit him with a flurry of punches that left several large knots on Jumper Jim's head.

Jake was in a killing rage. He fingered the handle on his skinning knife, partially pulling the blade from its scabbard. He finally got back in control and shoved the knife back in the its sheath. Jake took a few deep breaths before addressing the dazed men, "I don't know where you boys are from, but around here we treat our women folk with respect. The next time I hear you disrespect another woman will be the last time you do it!" Jake stomped out of the bar. It took him some time to calm down.

When the Tinker Gang regained their feet, the barkeep said, "You boys almost bought the farm. I guess you don't know that was Jake Jackson. I ain't never seen him that riled. Y'all are lucky to still have your hair!" As the Tinker Gang stumbled out of the door, Elwood threatened, "I don't care who that sum bitch is. He's going to get his!"

After a month of seeing Anne on a regular basis, Jake walked up to her front door nervous as a long tailed cat in a room full of rocking chairs. He wiped the sweat off the palms of his hands before knocking. Anne greeted him with a hug and a kiss, "It's good to see you, darling. I hate it when we miss a day of seeing each other like yesterday. It makes the day so unbearably long."

Jake opened his mouth to say something, but no words came out. Anne got a quizzical look on her face, "Jake, is there something wrong? You look…I've never seen you this way. Are you sick?" Jake finally croaked out, "I'm not sick…but…I need to say something and I…" Anne reassured him, "Honey, you know you can say anything to me. I love you. Whatever it is, I'll understand." Finally Jake blurted out, "Will you marry me?"

Of all the thing Anne could have imagined that Jake was trying to say, a marriage proposal was at the bottom of the list. Anne turned white as she sat down on the closest chair. It was her turn to search for words, "Jake, there was a long time when I didn't know if I would ever recover from losing Bob. He was the only man I ever loved…until now. I have the same feelings for you as I had for him. I…I just need some time to think."

Jake responded, "I do understand your confusion. You're the first woman I've had these kinds of feelings for since Macy died. I wasn't sure what to do until Burk said I need to get my brand on you before someone else…I don't mean a real brand. Burk was just…" Anne interrupted with a smile, "I know what you mean. I get what Burk meant. I just love that man. He is such a character! You are lucky to have someone that special in your life."

Jake sat down next to her, "I am lucky to have him in my life. I'm even luckier to have you in my life. Take as much time as you need. This is a big decision. You need to get it right." Anne tenderly kissed Jake, "Thank you, honey. I appreciate you giving me a little space. I promise I won't keep you waiting long."

Later…

Later that night at the ranch, Burk asked, "Well…How did it go?" Jake replied, "I asked her. She wanted a little time to think it over." Burk exploded, "What? You have fiddle-farted around and someone else has his rope on her! If you let that girl get away, I ain't too old to take you to the woodshed!" Jake laughed, "Calm down, old man. You're gonna give yourself a heart attack! I think she will be my wife. She just wants to be sure." Burk grumbled, "It better be alright or it's gonna be me and you. A whole lotta me and just a little bit of you!" Jake never laughed harder in his life.

The next afternoon, Anne drove her buggy up to the big house at the four-sixes. Burk grinned, "Well howdy, Anne. I didn't think my day could get any better, but it just did!" Anne gave Burk a hug and kissed his forehead. She asked, "Is Jake around?" Burk replied, "No, he's seeing about the ranch. Jake likes to make sure nobody's rustling my cattle.

The boy seems to take it personal if I have any cows come up missing. He should be back directly. Sit down a spell. I ain't gonna let you leave until we have supper. I'll have Cookie fix something special." Annie patted his hand, "I'd love to stay for supper. Jake has bragged on how good a cook, Cookie is!"

Burk prodded, "So…anything special going on with you?" Anne giggled because she knew what Burk was getting at, "Now Burk, there are some news that have to be delivered in person. I couldn't let the cat out of the bag too soon. That wouldn't be right, would it?" Burk sighed, "No…I guess not." Burk searched the horizon, "Where is that boy when we need him?" Anne laughed again.

As Jake rode up to headquarters, he saw Anne's buggy in front of the house. His pulse quickened. Jake thought, "What the hell is wrong with me? I've fought Indians on the warpath and gone up against the fastest gunfighters in the Southwest without a second thought. Yet, when I'm around this woman, I have the nerves of a schoolgirl. I must be going loco."

Jake noticed Anne and Burk were watching him ride up. As he got closer, Burk got up and went in the house. When Jake stepped on the porch, Anne threw herself into his arms. She covered him in kisses as she said, "The answer is yes! A thousand times yes!" Jake was equally happy and relieved.

That Sunday afternoon, Jake and Anne went on another picnic to what had become their favorite spot, the little lake by the grove of cottonwoods. Anne was spreading the blanket as Jake lifted the food basket down from the buggy.

A rifle shot broke the tranquility of the peaceful scene. The bullet hit Jake in the shoulder spinning him to the ground. He began looking for targets. Jake whispered to Anne, "Take the buggy. Ride back to the house and get some help." Jake didn't really want help. He used that as a ploy to get Anne to safety.

As Jake laid down random cover fire, Anne leapt on the buggy. She slapped the reins on the horses back, shouting, "Get up!" The Tinker Gang had pulled back when they saw that Jake was only wounded and not dead. They had no desire to face Jake Jackson's gun.

Instead they were waiting on Anne as she tried to escape. They shot the horse causing the buggy to cartwheel. Anne struck the ground hard enough to knock her unconscious. Elwood grinned as he loaded the limp woman in the front of his saddle, "Now let Jackson come to us. We'll have a special welcome for him!"

Jake heard the gunshot from the direction where Anne was going. After exposing himself from behind one of the cottonwood trees and not drawing any gunfire, Jake hurried down the road in pursuit of Anne. When he came upon the dead horse and destroyed buggy, anger welled up in him. His determination to follow the kidnappers was interrupted by a wave of nausea and a spinning mind. Jake collapsed unconscious.

At dusk Burk muttered, "Clyde, I was expecting Jake and Anne for supper. They went for a little picnic at the lake by the cottonwoods. Would you go check on them?" The darker it became, the more worried Burk became. He strained in the darkness to try to catch a glimpse of someone, anyone! Finally Clyde appeared, walking his horse with a body across the saddle.

Clyde called out, "It's Jake! There was no sign of Miss Anne except for what was left of the buggy. Someone had shot their horse!" Burk was plainly afraid, "Is he alive?" Clyde replied, "Yes, but he's lost a lot of blood!" Burk was glad to see that the bullet had passed through. Jake came to for a moment, he demanded, "Let me up! I've got to go see about Anne!" Burk responded, "Jake, you've lost too much blood. You couldn't ride a horse without falling off. I'll send Clyde and some of the boys to find Anne." Jake lapsed back into unconsciousness.

Clyde and three of the four-sixes' hands followed the distinct tracks of the three horses. Clyde felt they were gaining ground when a barrage of gunfire cut down all four cowboys. Elwood finished off two of them who were still alive with a bullet to the head. He pulled out a gagged Anne to see what happens when someone crosses him, "What do you think, missy? Get a good look at what we're gonna do to your boyfriend if he shows up." Anne was bleeding from a cut on her forehead. She spat and said, "You're an animal. When Jake gets here, he's going to take you apart!" Elwood slapped the defenseless girl hard, leaving a bruise on her face.

When Jake woke up the next morning, he asked Burke, "Any news on Anne?" Burk sighed deeply, "Yes, but it ain't good…Clyde's horse came in last night…without Clyde." Jake staggered when he tried to rise. Burk protested, "Son, it ain't gonna do no good. You're too weak to go after her!"

Jake swore, "Burk, I swear to God, if you don't help me get on Buck, I'll leave here and never come back!"

Burk could see there was no use in arguing. He helped Jake get dressed. Jake was able to saddle Buck, but Burk had to help him into the saddle. Burk said, "Be careful." Jake began to feel better. It did him good to be up and around.

Jake found the spot where Clyde and the boys had been murdered. The buzzards circling the bodies led him to them. Jake knew that the buzzards would also bring others from the four-sixes to fetch the bodies for burial. He spoke over Clyde's body, "You were a good man. You didn't deserve to die like this...the boys, too. I promise y'all that I'll bring your killers to justice. Rest in peace."

Finding Anne

Elwood had stripped Anne of all her clothing and tied her naked to a tree. The thorns of the mesquite tree punished her. Elwood, Jumper Jim and Hog would put their hands on her lasciviously enjoying the feel of her flesh. None of them actually assaulted Anne, preferring to humiliate her. She suffered the indignities of being treated like a subhuman. Anne never knew that there was this level of embarrassment. The truth was Elwood had never been with a woman despite his claims to the contrary. He was actually afraid of women. Elwood was afraid of a lot of things.

Anne had quit protesting the way she was being treated. She had grew weary of being beaten. Also her kidnappers had not fed her. Anne realized they didn't intend for her to survive. Elwood taunted her, "Where is the great Jake

Jackson? I don't see him! Do you suppose he's already found another woman, some other whore?"

Jake stepped out into an opening in the mesquite thicket. He declared, "If you're looking for me, here I am." Jake wasn't interested in further conversation. He pulled his Colt and began firing. The first bullet blew off Elwood's lower jaw.

Hog bowed his pig-like neck and charged Jake. The slug entered the crown of Hog's lowered head. It burrowed its way into Hog's skull making jelly out of his brain. Hog flopped on the ground with his fat legs kicking in unison with the dying quivers.

Jumper Jim had fallen to his knees pleading for mercy, "Please, Mr. Jackson, I never touched her. I was planning to help her escape!" Jake looked at Anne for confirmation. She disgustedly shook her head no. Jake put a slug between Jumper Jim's eyes. Red blood, gray brain matter and small, white, jagged pieces of his skull painted the mesquites and tumbleweeds.

Jake quickly retrieved a blanket from his saddle. He gently cut Anne loose and tenderly wrapped her in the blanker. Anne collapsed in Jake's arms. She had not shed a tear despite her mistreatment. Anne began to cry on Jake's shoulder. Jake stroked her hair and murmured, "I am so sorry, Anne. I should have protected you, but I didn't. I hope you can forgive me." Anne smiled through her tears, "Honey, this was not your fault. None of this was your fault! I believed in you. Even during the worst, I believed in you. I knew you would come...and you did!"

Jake had given a brief consideration to scalping these lowlifes, but thought it might be too much for Anne with everything she has been through. Anne already had a pretty good read on her future husband. She knew he was known to take scalps. Anne could tell he was giving it some thought.

A low moan interrupted their moment together. Elwood was still alive. Anne held out her hand to Jake, "Knife." A bewildered Jake handed her his skinning knife. Anne jerked on a handful of Elwood's hair. She proceeded to saw off a piece of his scalp. Elwood flinched and moaned louder with the pain of losing part of his scalp. Anne spit on the scalp and threw it back into Elwood's face. She handed the knife back to Jake and said, "Gun." Jake dutifully gave her his Colt. Anne emptied the pistol into Elwood's body. Anne asked as she handed the gun back to Jake, "How'd I do?" Jake grinned, "I couldn't have done it any better myself."

When Jake and Anne had gotten safely back to the ranch, Jake put her to bed to rest and heal. He and Burk drank coffee well into the night. Jake was apologetic, "Burk, you know I didn't mean what I said about leaving here?" Burk replied, "I knowed at the time you didn't mean it. You was riled up over that gal. Never gave it a second thought." Later, Jake told Burk about Anne scalping and shooting the outlaw. Jake wondered if Burk would ever stop laughing. With tears rolling down his face, Burk gasped, "I'll tell you one thing, boy. You better watch your ass around her!" The next day Anne asked, "I heard Burk laughing last night. What was he laughing at?" Jake snorted, "Who knows what makes that old coot laugh?"

It wouldn't be accurate to say Satana was a Kiowa renegade. He was just a flat-out renegade. Being Kiowa didn't have anything to do with it. Satana had no noble intentions for his acts of violence. He wasn't defending his tribe from injustice. Satana's only interest was himself.

When he jumped the reservation, a Cavalry captain asked Chief Sitting Wolf, "Do you have any idea why Satana went on the prod?" The Chief stiffened, "Satana does not walk the way of a true Kiowa. An evil spirit might know. Have your medicine man ask it." Sitting Wolf returned to his tipi. Satana had killed men and violated women of his own tribe. The people were glad to see him go.

Arkansas was suffering from a two year drought. Dan Long was weary and desperate from the struggle of trying to get enough from his small vegetable farm to feed his family. Dan sighed, "Gretchen, I think we have to face the facts. We're not going to make it here. You know how much I love Molly and Jenny, but having twin babies have strained us even more." Gretchen replied, "Honey, I know it's been hard. Adding two more mouths to feed made it even harder. When I married you, it was for richer or poorer. I meant that on our wedding day. It's still true today."

Dan plopped down on the wooden chair at their small table. He looked at the plate of cornbread. They had eaten only cornbread for the last two weeks. Dan suggested, "I hear there's land for the taking over in Texas. It's just a matter of time before this place will be sold for the back taxes. We might want to think about pulling up stakes and becoming Texicans." Gretchen grinned, "I ain't sure what a Texican is, but I'd be willing to try it if you think that's what we should do." Dan leaned over the crib, "Well what about it, girls? You want to become Texicans too?" Molly and Jenny laughed as their father tickled them.

Dan scowled as he was deep in thought. Gretchen put her hand on his shoulder, "What?" Dan sighed deeply, "I just can't seem to come up with a way to get the money for the trip to Texas." Gretchen disappeared but reappeared in a minute. She extended her hand. Dan protested, "No Gretchen! Your mother gave you that broach! I know what it means to you. I'll think of another way."

Gretchen smiled, "Honey, you know as well as I do that there is no other way. I wore it to town once. Mrs. Green at the mercantile admired it. She said if I ever wanted to sell it, she would buy it. The broach is important to me, but not as important as my family. My family comes first!"

When the Longs explained to Mrs. Green why they needed to sell the broach, she overpaid for it making sure Dan, Gretchen and their adorable babies had enough cash to finance relocating to Texas. Dan was able to buy a serviceable wagon and horse that could withstand the trip to Texas. Dan and Gretchen packed the wagon with their meager belongings, foodstuffs and Dan's old military, percussion muzzle loader. They made a pallet in a corner of the wagon for the babies. The next morning they headed for Texas.

Dan slapped the reins on the horse urging him forward. He grinned as he looked at this wife, "Here we go! I have to admit I'm a little excited. It's hard to describe the feeling of discovering new country!" Gretchen squeezed his arm as she sat by him on the wagon seat, "I'm excited too! I hope our new home will be a good place to raise Molly and Jenny. We're all going to be Texicans!" Dan laughed as he looked back to check on the babies.

They stopped at several farms and ranches along the way. Everyone advised that a family like theirs could homestead 160 acres along the Brazos River in central Texas. At the end of their long journey, Dan pulled up on a ridge overlooking a small valley nestled in a crook of the Brazos. He asked Gretchen, "What do you see?" Gretchen replied, "I'm not sure, but it's beautiful...I give up. What do I see?" Dan smiled, "You're looking at our new home." Gretchen gasped, "Oh, honey! It's more than I could have asked! We are going to be so happy!"

The next two weeks were filled with building a sod home from bricks chopped from the prairie. When it was finished, Dan and Gretchen stepped back to admire the modest, earthen shelter. Gretchen exclaimed, "I bet the Governor of Texas doesn't live in a nicer home than ours!" Dan hugged his wife in agreement.

Dan had brought his farming tools from Arkansas. He now busied himself with busting sod to plant crops. One day Dan unexpectedly hurried back in the house. He quickly retrieved his rifle that was leaning in the corner. Gretchen was worried, "Dan, what is it?" Dan held the rifle in one hand and scratched his head with the other, "I ain't rightly sure...It's more of a feeling than anything else. I heard a noise then all the birds stopped chirping...It made my skin crawl." Gretchen whispered, "Oh Dan! What do you think it is?" Dan set his jaw, "Only one way to find out."

Dan slowly opened the door built from the wooden scraps from the wagon. He carefully looked around before stepping outside. Gretchen heard a loud thump. Dan staggered then toppled backward. Only the fletching from the arrow could be seen protruding from his chest. Gretchen screamed as she looked into the sightless eyes of her husband. Gretchen scrambled to pick up the rifle. Satana put his foot on the gun pinning it to the ground. Gretchen began to beg, "Please! Please don't hurt my babies! I'll do anything you want, just leave them alone!"

In the end no amount of pleading swayed Satana. He put the babies under the knife and used Gretchen for the better part of two days before slitting her throat. At that point Gretchen welcomed death. Satana was in a murderous rage. That week he killed 14 men, women and children whose only crime was living along the peaceful Brazos.

Burke was overjoyed at the news that Jake and Anne were getting married. He offered, "Unless y'all got your heart set on a church wedding, how about having the wedding here. I'll throw the biggest shindig that's ever been seen in these parts!" Jake looked at Anne. Anne replied, "Burk, we'd be forever grateful if we could get married here." Burk responded, "Hot damn!" Jake added, "The only thing is I don't know about the shindig part. I ain't much for shindigs." Burk retorted, "Shut up, boy! Don't you know nothing? This wedding don't have anything to do with you! It's what she wants that counts. Just be glad she's letting you tag along."

Over Supper

Over supper that night, Burk eyed Jake and Anne cautiously, "So…you two given any thought where you're gonna live after you get hitched?" Anne said, "Well…there's always my house in town." Jake looked like he had just swallowed cow manure. Burk replied, "Honey, if you don't mind me saying so, civilized folks aren't going to cotton living next to a heathen like Jake. They might develop a bad case of the drizzling's." Anne laughed, "Burk, I just love you!...Well what would you suggest?"

Burk pretended to be thinking when he knew all along what he was going to say. He swept his arm around the room, "What about here? This old house is way too big for an old man like me. There's plenty of room. You wouldn't hardly know I was here. In fact you wouldn't hear a peep out of me!" Jake snorted, "Not hear a peep out of you? That'll be the day!" Anne smiled, "One good thing about living here is the two of you would definitely keep me entertained!" Anne looked at Jake, "What do you think? I guess I knew I wouldn't be able to keep you cooped up in town."

Later when Jake went to check on Buck, Burk sat down next to Anne and held her hand between his, "I know you know I don't have children or any family except for Jake. I also know you don't have any family either. So, I was just wondering…thinking…maybe, you might think of me as your Pa?" Tears welled up in Anne's eyes, "I would like that just fine…Pa." When Jake came back from the barn, he found Anne and Burk holding hands and crying. Jake thought, "What the hell? I wasn't gone that long."

Burk kept his promise. The wedding between Jake and Anne was indeed a shindig. Folks came from miles around. There was so much food, Burk insisted when anyone left the party they had to take a platter of brisket with them. When the preacher asked for their "I do's", it was a tossup who cried more Anne or Burk. Later when Jake gave Burk a questioning look, Burk retorted, "I had something in my eye! Can't a man get something in his eye? You just need to tend to your own knitting!"

When Anne and Jake kissed at the end of the ceremony, Anne whispered, "For a while I had given up on ever being happy again. Thank you, honey for making me so happy!" Jake replied, "One of us needs to be thanking the other one, but you don't need to be thanking me. I need to be thanking you. Anne, you've given my life meaning again. Thank you for that."

Satana watched the cowboys brand the calves for a long time. Like a wolf watching a herd of deer, he was waiting for an opportunity to catch one of the white eyes by themselves. Thad, the new foreman at the four-sixes, stated, "Chester, this branding is a bigger chore than I thought it was going to be. Ride over to the south pasture. Bring a couple of the boys back to help out." Chester mounted his horse. He said to Thad, "It's only a couple of miles. I'll be back shortly." Chester put his horse in a short lope.

The arrow slammed into the belly of the horse. The horse squealed, bucked and mule-kicked. Chester was caught unawares. He was pitched head first, striking his head on a rock. When Chester regained consciousness, he found himself staked out. His arms and legs were spread. Chester had been stripped of his clothes with his shirt stuffed in his mouth as a gag. Satana leered at the helpless cowboy with an evil glint in his eye. Chester looked on in terror as Satana brandished his knife. The Kiowa slowly began to peel the skin from Chester's body. His screams were muffled by the gag.

Thad scratched his head, "Chester should have been back with the boys by now. Finish branding that calf and put out the fire. We're going to look for him." One of the men asked, "All of us?" Thad nodded his head, "Yeah, I reckon we'll all go." Thad didn't mention what he was thinking, because there hadn't been any Indian trouble for years. The hairs on the back of his neck were standing up. It was the same feeling he used to get whenever hostile Indians were close.

The cowboys rode up on the horrific scene. Their friend had been skinned alive. One of the hands bent over to the side of his horse to vomit. Thad would never eat another squirrel or rabbit after that day. Their skinned bodies reminded Thad of how Chester looked. Thad choked, "Let's get a blanket on Chester. We need to carry him back to headquarters."

Jake had just come in from making a round checking on rustlers. He knew it was highly unusual for that many men coming in during that time of day. Jake saw the body draped across one of the horses. He started walking toward them.

Thad exclaimed, "Indians!" Jake replied, "Thad, are you sure? I hadn't heard any reports of any raiding parties breaking out of the reservation." Thad responded, "I couldn't believe it either. It's been several years since we've had any hostiles. Take a look at Chester's body. Only one thing could have done that."

Burk answered, "I don't think it's a raiding party. Ain't heard nothing about that. I have heard there's a renegade Kiowa who's been raising holy hell. He ain't done anything around here. It's probably him. They say his name is Satana and he's muy malo."

Jake started gathering his gear. Anne said fearfully, "Jake, you're not going after him, are you? You heard Burk say he was a dangerous man!" Jake replied, "So am I."

Anne and Burk watched Jake saddle Buck. He rode off with a wave. Anne said softly, "Pa, he's going to be alright, isn't he?" Burk responded with a reassuring arm around her shoulders, "Don't fret none. Jake can take care of hisself. You should be more worried about the Indian dying than Jake."

Jake lost Satana's tracks several times. Satana didn't travel in a straight line. He went out of his way to ride down creeks or rocky ground. Jake thought, "I'll say one thing for this Kiowa. He is good. The only one who could track him is another Indian."

Satana was so confident that he couldn't be followed, he was roasting a jackrabbit on a spit. Satana figured no white man could trail him. He knew an Indian wouldn't. Satana was startled when a booming voice said in perfect Kiowa, "You have come a long way to die here!" Jake stepped out where Satana could see him.

Satana smirked, "I see you have a gun. I have no gun. Why don't you fight me with a knife like a true warrior?" Jake laughed, "You are not a Kiowa warrior who demands respect. I have known great Kiowa warriors. You are not fit to lick their feet." Satana replied, "You must be the one the Comanche dogs call White Wolf. Today my knife will feast on your blood. Do you accept my challenge?"

Jake slowly shook his head, "I do not accept your challenge. You have no honor and do not deserve a warrior's death. There is a second reason. It would piss off my squaw." Faster than most human eyes could follow, Jake drew and fired his Colt. The bullet poked a hole squarely in the middle of Satana's chest. It was a killing shot for most men. Instead Satana screamed a war cry and charged Jake. A second slug knocked the Indian to the ground. Quick as a cat, fueled by hatred and blood lust, Satana sprang back to his feet determined to kill the white man. A third shot took off the top of Satana's skull putting him down for good.

Jake had no respect for those who kill without good reason. He scalped Satana. Jake dismembered the body and scattered the parts. He smiled, "The coyotes and buzzards will eat well today."

Upon his return, the hands first noticed the scalp hanging from Jake's saddle. Word quickly spread that the Indian problem was over. Anne was in Jake's arms before he could unsaddle Buck. She laughed, "I never thought a scalp would bring me happiness." Jake noticed that Buck not only tolerated Anne, he bent his neck so she could scratch between his ears. Jake grinned when he spoke to

Buck, "I see she's got you under her spell too." Jake and Anne walked arm in arm to the house for supper.

Texas Rose

Laura Bullion was born in Tom Green County in Texas. Her mother was of German descent and died giving birth to Laura. Her father was unknown as her mother was briefly captured by the Comanche. When she escaped, she was with child. Later in life, Laura became infamously known as Texas Rose. Texas Rose was the only woman who ran an outlaw gang during this period of Texas.

Rose was a striking woman. She had an exotic look with her German/Comanche cross. Rose hated the fact that on the whole, men were created physically stronger women. Men were deferred to by women. That made Rose sick, "Why should I do what some man wants me to do just cause he's a man? Most men are idiots who can't see past their own crotch!"

Rose quickly learned that she could use her sex as an advantage instead of allowing it to be a liability. One of her first seductions was an outlaw named Red Slocum. Red chewed tobacco with a constant juice stain down the front of his shirt. No one knew when the last time Red had a bath. Some thought it was a day that his horse went bronco and threw him in the creek. Those who were there claimed they saw several fish turn belly up and die.

Despite Red being filthy, Rose held her nose because he had something she wanted, a ready-made gang of four outlaws. In less than a week, Red was following Rose around like a puppy dog. She began giving the orders instead of Red. He let her do whatever she wanted as long as she ended up in his bedroll.

Rose told Red, "For God sakes, go take you a bath!" Red was bewildered, "But Rose, honey, I had me a good washin' when my horse dumped me in the creek!"

The Slocum Gang specialized in robbing stagecoaches. Rose changed up the way they operated on the next holdup. After the gang killed the guard and shot the driver, two elderly, white-haired passengers stepped out of the coach. Benny Smith pleaded, "You're welcome to our valuables. Just leave me and the missus be and we'll be on our way."

In the past Red would have let them go free. The blast from the Colt startled Red. Rose put two bullets into Mr. and Mrs. Smith. Red protested, "Now Rose, why come you done that? Them folks gave up their poke!" Rose replied with a slug from her Colt right between Red's eyes. Red flopped on the ground for a bit before dying. She addressed the rest of the gang, "I'm running this gang from here on out! Is that a problem for anybody?"

The gang members were not exactly deep thinkers. They followed Red's orders. They didn't see much difference in following Rose's. Rose stated, "The driver's only wounded...kill him. While you're at it, kill the horses too. As long as I'm ramrodding this outfit, we don't leave any loose ends. No witnesses! Killing the horses makes the law come look for the stage. That buys us more time for our get-a-way."

Rose was smart enough to realize that the law would eventually catch up to her and her gang if they camped out in open country. She thought, "I need me a place where I can appear to be respectable…a respectable headquarters." Rose asked her boys over a campfire one night, "What's the nicest saloon you bunch of yahoos ever been in? I mean some place that was respectable enough that the likes of you might get thrown out."

The boys weren't used to being asked questions. They just wanted to be told who to rob and kill. Finally Floyd said, "The classiest joint I was ever in was the Palace in San Antonio. The little brass bowls you spit into was all nice and shiny! I figured a King or something must have owned the place." Charley chimed in, "I been there once. The sum bitch was real nice! The girls were purdy. I figured I didn't have enough money to get one of them so I left." In a few minutes, Floyd asked, "Are we gonna go to San Antonio and visit the Palace?" Rose responded, "Hell, no! We're going to go to San Antonio and I'm going to buy the Palace!"

Rose shoved through the batwing doors of the Palace. She gawked at the ceiling. It was the first time she'd ever seen a chandelier. Rose pushed through the crowd at the bar. The barkeep eyed the tough looking woman and the derelicts who seemed to be guarding her. The bartender's raised eyebrow told Rose that she and the boys weren't the kind of clientele who frequented the Palace.

Rose slapped the bar with the palm of her, waking the bartender from his trance, "Mister, do you see me standing here? Give me and the boys a couple bottles of whiskey…Do you hear me? Move!" The other patrons at the bar began to move away. Instead of using shot glasses, Rose just passed the bottles around. One of her men had to elbow Floyd because he wasn't passing the bottle fast enough.

Rose asked the bartender, "Who owns this joint?" The bartender replied, "Mr. John Walker is the proprietor." Rose responded, "If that means owner, tell him Rose Bullion is here to see him." The bartender stated, "Mr. Walker normally only entertains guests by invitation. I'm sure he is quite busy." Rose reached across the bar, grabbing the bartender by the front of his shirt, "You go tell Walker that I'm here to pay cash for this saloon. He won't like it if I have to go look for him!" The bartender noticed the four saddle bums all had their hands on the butts of their pistols. He reluctantly nodded, "Very well, madam. I will see if he's available."

Instead of waiting, Rose and her boys followed the bartender to a back office. Just before he knocked, the bartender realized he had been followed, "Now look, you aren't allowed back here!" Rose brushed by him and opened the door. John Walker was surprised, "Can I help you?" Two burly men with sawed-off shotguns flanked the saloon owner.

Rose laughed, "Actually, I come to help you. I'm here to buy your saloon...cash money on the barrelhead!" After taking a minute to digest what just happened, Walker responded, "First, I doubt you have the money to buy the Palace. You probably can't count that high. Second, if I wanted to sell the Palace which I don't, what makes you think I would sell something as fine as the Palace to a half-breed like you?" The two bodyguards had already leveled their shotguns at Rose and her gang. Rose held up one hand

and smiled, "Okay, have it your way…but, you'll regret not taking my offer!"

Rose and her boys watched from the concealment of a dark alley as one of Walker's bodyguards pulled up to a side door driving a buggy. They followed the buggy to Walker's mansion on the outskirts of San Antonio. Before gaining entry to the house, Rose whispered, "Kill the guards, but do not kill Walker. If one of you accidently kills Walker, you die with him."

Walker had already gone to sleep when one of the bodyguards heard glass break from the back of the house. Rose was waiting for him when he came to investigate. She whispered, "Open your mouth, you die. Keep it closed, you live." Rose told Floyd, "Tie him up and gag him…Charley, you and the rest of the boys come with me." Rose found the second bodyguard asleep on the couch. She cracked him on the skull with the butt of her Colt, sending him into a deeper sleep.

Walker woke up when someone was punching him in the shoulder. When he could focus, he was looking down the barrel of Rose's Colt. Walker sputtered, "Wh..what..what's the meaning of this outrage? Are you insane? Don't you know who I am?" Rose laughed, "I know who you are. You're the man who's about to sell me the Palace." Walker retorted, "Over my dead body!" Rose put the barrel up against his temple, "That can be arranged."

After tying him up, Floyd led him into the living room, shoving him down on the couch next to his trussed up bodyguards. Rose announced, "Here's the deal. You're gonna get the deed to the Palace wherever you got it hid and sign it over to me." Walker retorted, "I will not!" Rose said, "Charley." Charley jerked down Walker's pants and held a knife to his private parts. Walker desperately asked his guards, "Aren't you going to do something?" The look on their faces said they were helpless to do anything.

The knife started to cut into his manhood. Walker screamed, "Alright! Alright! I'll do it!" Walker retrieved the deed from his safe. He signed it over to Rose. The only one of Rose's boys who could write his own name was Floyd. Floyd signed the document as the witness. Rose folded the deed, "Now see all the trouble you caused? It would have been so much simpler if you had taken me up on my offer to begin with." Rose laughed because she knew that even if Walker had agreed that night, the outcome would have been the same. She wasn't about to pay good money for something she could just take.

Charley gagged Walker. He and the rest of the boys loaded the saloon owner and his bodyguards in the back of the buggy after harnessing the horse. Floyd tied his horse to the rear of the buggy. Floyd popped the buggy whip and pointed the horse west. Rose took the lead. The rest of the gang followed closely. It was rough going with the buggy across the prairie. Rose didn't want to risk encountering people by using the roads.

Finally Rose found what she was looking for, a sandy, creek bed. It would make the digging easy. After the boys untied the shovels from their saddles, they dug a hole big enough for three bodies. Rose ordered, "Take their gags off. Ain't nobody could hear em out here. Bring them over here next to the hole." Walker objected, "Why are you doing this? I give you what you want! You wanted the Palace. You got it all legal like! What else do you want?" The burly body guards were crying like little girls.

Rose smirked, "You want to know what I want? I'll tell you what I want. I want no loose ends! Boys, kill those two, but bury Walker alive for shaming me at the Palace." All three men died screaming.

Rose filed the deed to the Palace at the county courthouse. Local citizens demanded a thorough investigation of the disappearance of John Walker. The Sheriff told everyone who asked, "I don't know what happened to Walker. We followed tracks leading west, but eventually lost them on bedrock. All I know is for some reason that nobody knows, he sold the Palace to Rose Bullion. I pulled the deed at the courthouse. It was legal. That's all I know."

Rose smiled as she surveyed her saloon. She briefly thought about renaming it the Texas Rose, but decided that the reputation of the Palace was too valuable. The bartender rushed up to her, "Ma'am, I hope there's no hard feelings about the other night. I was just trying to do my job." Rose replied, "There's no hard feelings. The problem is you let me go back to where I wasn't supposed to go. If that was doing your job, you are piss poor at it. You're fired!"

Rose gave Floyd a roll of money, "You and the boys go across the street to the mercantile. Outfit everybody in new duds. Don't let anyone put them on until you come back over here and take a bath. Get some of the girls to pour you baths. You can't be representing me no more looking and smelling like that!" Floyd hesitated, "Rose about the girls...me and the boys...well, we were wondering..." Rose cut him off, "Y'all can pick one girl each. You can have five minutes with her. No more than that! Every minute she's wasting with you, is costing me money."

When Floyd told the others, Charley exclaimed, "Sum bitch! We done struck it rich! Store bought clothes, indoor baths and our very own whore! I guess the luckiest day in our lives was the day Rose plugged ol' Red!"

The next week, Rose called a meeting in her new office. She said, "This saloon makes more money than I thought it would. That might be enough for some. It ain't enough for me! There's stagecoaches, trains, banks and rich folks that have money for the taking! I'm gonna take all I can get! Maybe if I can get enough money, I might become the first woman Governor of Texas!"

Floyd grinned, "That sure sounds might fine...Rose if you were the governor, do you suppose you might...oh, I donno...maybe double our time with the girls to ten minutes?" The rest of the gang looked on hopefully. Rose spit, "Men! For the life of me, I don't understand why women don't already own everything!"

Five Card Stud

Charles "Slick" Crawford sat at the poker table dealing 5 card stud. Slick had wavy blonde hair and eyes that some ladies claimed were bluer than the sky itself. The capper was his brilliant smile with pearly white teeth. His smile reportedly caused some women to buckle at the knees.

Rose did a double-take the first time she laid eyes on Slick. Her dalliance with Red had soured Rose on men. Rose watched him for quite some time before introducing herself. She smiled as she extended her hand, "Hello, I'm Rose Bullion. As the owner of the Palace, I wanted to welcome you." Slick flashed his smile. Instead of shaking her hand, Slick kissed the back of it, "It is my pleasure to make the acquaintance of such a beautiful creature. Surely, you are what God had in mind when he created Eve. My name is Charles Crawford, but my friends call me Slick. I hope you'll call me Slick."

Rose blushed as she felt the heat rush to her face. She wanted to reply, but her tongue would not cooperate. Finally Rose blurted out, "Sir, the pleasure is mine. If there's anything you need, just let me know. I'll see to it." Rose told her new bartender, "Whatever Mr. Crawford wants, it's on the house. Tell him it's with the compliments of Rose Bullion."

Later that night, Slick accepted an invitation to supper in Rose's private room upstairs. After the meal, Slick asked with a devilish glint in his eye, "Rose, that may be the best steak I've ever eaten. What's next?" Rose sat down in his lap. She put her arms around his neck and purred, "Whatever you want, honey. Whatever you want." After that first night, Rose and Slick were inseparable. The employees of the Palace began treating Slick as an owner.

Eventually Rose called a meeting with her gang. Slick was in attendance. Rose stated, "Slick, the saloon makes money, but I make much more robbing stagecoaches and trains with these boys. Are you shocked to hear that?" Slick smiled his famous smile, "Not at all. It just confirms what I thought. Rose Bullion, you are one helluva business woman!"

The Letter

Anne excitedly waved the letter at Jake, "This was waiting for me at the post office! It's from my old friend, Cheryl Mathis. Cheryl and I went to school together. We lost touch when she married and moved to Kansas City. She wants to come for a visit! Burk has already said he would love to meet her. What do you think?" Jake laughed at seeing Anne so happy, "Of course, I would love to meet her too. It might be interesting to see what you were like in school!" Anne responded, "Oh, hush! I'm going to send Cheryl a wire to make the arrangements. I can't wait to see her!"

Jake and Anne were waiting at the stagecoach yard in Ft. Worth for Cheryl's arrival. Anne kept straining her eyes trying to get the first glimpse of the stage. Anne's spirits went progressively downhill the later the stage became. Anne sighed, "It's two hours overdue. It should have been here by now!" Jake had ridden Buck while Anne drove the buggy to make sure there was plenty of room for Cheryl's luggage.

Jake squeezed Anne's shoulder, "I'm going to ride Buck to meet the stage. They might have had some kind of trouble. It's not unusual to bust a wheel. Maybe I can be of some help." Anne pleaded, "Jake, please go find her." Jake replied, "Will you be alright here?" Anne patted the Colt in her purse, "I'll be fine."

Jake found the stage. It was just south of the Red River. He grimly surveyed the remains of the holdup. The bodies of the driver and guard were riddled with bullet holes. The woman had been shot in the head at close range. He wrapped the woman's body in his blanket and tied it behind Buck's saddle. Jake reluctantly started for Ft. Worth. He dreaded facing Anne.

Anne screamed, "No! it can't be!...Jake, maybe it's not her. Let me see!" Jake firmly held his wife, "Anne, it's her. There was only one woman...She would be hard to identify. I brought her purse. The thieves emptied it of money, but there's the wire you sent her about coming here."

Jake loaded the blood-soaked blanket containing Cheryl's body in the back of the buggy. Jake hitched Buck to the rear of the buggy. Buck hated to be led like that, but somehow he sensed something was wrong. Buck followed the buggy back to the ranch.

Jake held Anne that night while she cried herself to sleep. They buried Cheryl in the ranch graveyard the next morning. Afterwards, Anne sat in one of the chairs on the porch. She vacantly stared off into space. Jake and Burk decided to give her some space and time to grieve.

That afternoon Anne called out, "Jake, come here please." Jake sat down in a chair next to hers and held her hand. There was a hard look on Anne's face, "Jake, I want you to find who killed Cheryl. Find them and bring them to justice! If you can bring them in for trial, that would be fine. Do whatever needs to be done. If you have to kill them then kill them. I don't care if they leave this world with hair or without hair. Make those animals pay for what they done!"

After Jake had saddled Buck and packed provisions, he kissed Anne and shook Burk's hand. Anne and Burk watched him ride out of sight. Anne gasped with the finality of the situation, "Pa, I think I have made a big mistake! I sent the man I love to face killers. What have I done?" Burk slipped his arm around Anne's shoulders, "Don't fret none, child. That ain't just any man. Remember, you're married to Jake Jackson."

Jake started at the scene of the holdup. The outlaws didn't retreat in a straight line. They tried to use the surrounding countryside to confuse anyone trying to follow them. The creeks, rocky ground and a few rivers would have thrown off most pursuers. Jake's tracking skill was developed as a boy living with the Comanche. Red Elk used to praise his adopted son's ability to track something that other Comanche could not.

After a couple of weeks on the trail, Jake pulled up Buck to stare at the outskirts of San Antonio.

Gambling

The poker played jumped to his feet, knocking over his chair, "Mister, that's too many hands in a row that the last card won for you!" Slick smiled, "Simmer down, cowboy. I'll buy you a beer. I want us to remain friends." The cowboy swore, "We ain't friends, sum bitch! I wouldn't be friends with a four-flushing, cheating bottom-dealer like you...I want my money back!" The cowboy started to draw his gun, ready to enforce his demand.

Slick had already pulled his pistol. He held it at the ready under the table. Slick shot through the table, blasting a hole where the cowboy's heart used to be. The cowboy staggered before pitching forward on the table. Slick exclaimed, "Dammit, just look at that! I hate it when blood gets all over the cards and the money!"

Rose asked, "Slick, honey, can I have a word with you in private?" Slick scooped up his money and followed Rose to the back. In her office Rose said, "Slick, do you know how much money we have?" Slick replied, "Well, not exactly. But I know it's a bunch." Rose raised her voice, "It is more than a bunch. We got enough money that you don't need to be cheating at cards! For God's sake, let em win a hand once in a while!" Slick grinned, "Darling, it's just...it's just all that money sitting there for the taking. You of all people should understand that."

Rose tapped a foot before sighing, "Well...Oh hell, I can't stay mad at you." When Slick started to hug her, Rose pushed him away, "And don't think I don't know what goes on between you and some of the girls! Keep it in your pants or I will shoot it off!" Despite her resistance, Slick embraced and kissed Rose, "Now darling, you know you're the only one I love. I only have eyes for you!" Rose responded, "It ain't your eyes that are gonna get you in trouble."

Over the long days of tracking the outlaws' horses, one set of tracks stood out. That particular horse had a front hoof that turned slightly to the right. Jake followed that track until it ended at a big bay tied to the hitching rail in front of the Palace. A quick examination of the right front confirmed what Jake already knew. He patted the horse on the neck, "I'll just wait across the street until your owner comes to claim you." Jake and Buck hid in the shadows of an alley.

Rose and bought a small house close to the edge of town. She wanted her boys staying there until it was time for another job. Rose ordered, "You boys can drink at the Palace as long as you pay with your own money. You're welcome to the girls as long as you pay with your own money. They ain't nothing free just because you work for me! I want you staying nights at the house I bought for you."

A drunken Floyd staggered out of the Palace. He tried to mount the bay. It took him three tries to get on its back. Floyd muttered, "I believe he's still growing. This sum bitch gets harder to get on every day." Floyd passed out across his bed. Jake dented his skull with the butt of his Colt to make sure he stayed passed out. There was a small canyon an hour west of San Antonio that Jake had picked out the day before.

Jake splashed water on Floyd's face. Floyd was groggy as he gained consciousness. As his focus became clearer, Floyd realized he was tied to a tree and something had happened to his clothes. A shiver of fear ran down Floyd's spine when he saw Jake, "What is this? Why am I here? What do you want?" When Jake didn't respond, Floyd panicked, "I got money...I know where I can get you lots more! Just tell me what you want! I'll get it for you!"

Jake smiled, "I'll tell you what I want. I want to know who you work with? I want to know who you work for? And let's save us both some time. I trailed your horse from the holdup of the stage south of the Red River. I saw the bodies of the two men and the woman that you killed. I know there are four of you. You don't look smart enough to plan as operation like this. That tells me there's someone else at the top pulling your string. You can make it easy on yourself by telling me everything I want to know. Otherwise it won't be pretty."

Floyd denied, "Mister...whatever your name is, you got the wrong guy. I ain't never robbed or killed nobody in my life!" Jake took his skinning knife and lopped off one of Floyd's fingers. Floyd screamed, "I'm telling you, mister. You got the wrong guy!" Jake cut off a second finger. Floyd begged, "Stop! I will tell you what you want!" Jake replied, "Let's hear it." Floyd sobbed, "My three pards are Charley, Jed and Tom. They live in the same house as me." Jake asked, "Who's running this sorry outfit?" Floyd answered, "It's just us. I'm the ramrod." Jake reached for a third finger. Floyd shouted, "Wait! I'll tell you. Rose Bullion who owns the Palace plans all our jobs. She's running with a card shark, Slick Crawford. Slick as dealt himself in on our deal."

Floyd took a breath and forced a grin, "I guess you'll let me go know that I told you what you wanted? That was our deal, right?" Jake shook his head, "No deal. I'm going to hang you." Floyd protested, "But you said you'd go easy on me! You promised!" Jake smiled, "I am going easy on you. I'm letting you keep the rest of your fingers and toes. See, that woman you shot was a good friend of my wife's. If I don't hang you, she might not speak to me for a week. I can't have that."

With his hands and feet tied, Floyd sobbed as Jake looped a noose around his neck. Jake threw the rope over the limb of an oak and slowly pulled Floyd off his feet. When Floyd quit kicking and jerking, Jake tied the rope to the tree trunk. Jake tipped his hat to Floyd, "I know you'll get right lonesome, but don't worry. I'm gonna bring you some company."

The next day Charley reported Floyd's disappearance to Rose and Slick. Slick stated, "I doubt it's anything to be concerned about. You know Floyd is a drunk. He's probably sleeping it off somewhere. He'll show up anytime now." Charley wasn't convinced. An uneasy feeling in the pit of his stomach told Charley that something bad had happened to Floyd.

The boys didn't go to the Palace the next night. They felt like they could better protect themselves by watching each other's backs at the house. Charley jumped and waved his gun, "What was that? Did you hear that noise?" Jed responded, "That weren't nothing! You're spooking at everything! We don't even know for sure that Floyd's dead. He could walk through that door any minute. Calm down and have a drink." Charley replied, "That's a good idea. I could use a little whiskey for my nerves."

A little whiskey turned into a lot. Soon all three men were passed out. Jake gave each a dose of his gun butt to keep their lights out. Floyd's pards woke up to the grisly specter of their old friend hanging, slightly swinging in the breeze. The moonlight revealed Floyd's face was black with his tongue hanging out of one side of his mouth.

The outlaws urinated in their pants. They begged for their lives. Jake face hardened, "You boys might ought to save your breath. In a few minutes you're going to need it…I do have some good news. I'm going to hang each of you with your own rope." After observing the outlaws receiving frontier justice, Jake oddly noted that it reminded him of a Christmas tree he once saw, the decorations dangling from its limbs. Jake spoke to Floyd, "I kept my word, ol' pard. Now you got company."

Rose woke from a sound sleep. There was something making her bed wet. She turned up the lamp. To her horror, Slick's throat was cut and his blood was soaking the bed. A gun cocked and the muzzle pressed against her head. Jake whispered, "I'd be quiet if I were you. My Colt has a hair trigger and I'm already a little nervous being in a strange woman's bedroom and all. I sure hope my wife doesn't find out about this."

Rose replied, "What do you want?" Jake responded, "The main thing is I just wanted you to know that your gang is dead. I hung em. I've heard all about how smart you were so I know you've already figured out that this snake lying beside you is also dead." Rose sat up. She let the sheet drop. She suggested, "Mister, I can be real nice to the right man. It looks like to me that you're the right man. We could go away together. I got enough money to last us a lifetime…What do you say, just you and me?"

Jake slowly shook his head, "That's a mighty fine offer, but that's just not me." Jake's hand moved faster than the eye can see. His blade sliced Rose's pretty neck from one of her delicate ears to the other. Jake gave Rose a red necklace to match her lover's. Some folks would separate dealing with a woman differently from a man. Jake believed that on some things, except when it came to outlaws. As far as he was concerned, every outlaw was treated the same, man or woman.

One of the hands ran up to the front door and knocked loudly. He yelled, "Jake's back!" Anne burst out of the door and beat the hand to the barn where Jake was unsaddling Buck. She sobbed, "I'm so sorry, honey! I can't believe I wanted you to go after those killers! I've regretted that every single day you've been gone! Please forgive me!" Jake gathered her in his arms, "There's nothing to forgive, sweetheart. That bunch needed to be brought to heel. Not only to be punished, but to keep them from hurting other folks…I know it won't bring her back, but I did get justice for Chery!"

Burk snorted, "What took you so long? We got work that needs to be done around here, you know!" Jake laughed, "I missed you too, Burk."

"Buckskin" Frank Warner was a notorious gunfighter and hired killer. When he was 18, a local bully forced Buckskin into his first gunfight at a saloon in Ft. Worth. The bully taunted, "Hey boy, that buckskin vest don't make you any faster with that hogleg you got on your hip! Everybody know I run The Greasy Spot. I've been letting you come in here for a couple of days. At first you was just a skeeter buzzing around. Now you're starting to piss me off. Let's see how fast you really are!"

The old Colt with its worn holster was the only possession that his Pa had when he died of consumption. Buckskin had fired it a couple of times. He couldn't afford to shoot it much. The shells were too expensive.

Buckskin couldn't explain it but he felt no fear at the challenge. He said matter of factly, "I'm ready when you are." The bully went for his gun. Before he could clear leather, he found himself facing the muzzle of Buckskin's Colt. The onlookers gasped at the speed of Buckskin's draw. The Colt just seemed to jump into Buckskin's hand. The bully started backing up, "Now hold on. I didn't mean nothing by what I said...Tell you what. I'll buy you a beer and we can be pards!"

Buckskin glanced around the bar before saying, "You started this. I'm gonna finish it." Buckskin coldly pulled the trigger. The .45 slug crashed through the bully's teeth and punched out the back of his head. Small shards of teeth and pools of blood joined the tobacco quid on the filthy floor.

Buckskin could feel the attitudes in the bar change from contempt to fear and respect. Buckskin stated, "I'm taking this man's gun and any money he's carrying. He don't need it no more. Any objections?" When no one spoke up, Buckskin added, "I need someone to point out his horse. I'm taking it too." As he rode away, it dawned on Buckskin that he could make money with a gun.

Arlin Nolen set his sights high. The Bar N wasn't much now, but Nolen was determined to build it into the largest ranch in the state of Texas.

He had won 1,000 acres in a rigged poker game. The former ranch owner shouted, "That ain't right. I ain't never heard of anyone loosing with four aces! You drawing that straight flush on the last card weren't luck! It was cheating, pure and simple!" Nolen's man shot the rancher in the back." Nolen stood over the dead body, "I see you met my man who handles all the complainers and whiners." Nolen was not satisfied with that. He wanted more…much more!

One of Nolen's boys called him off to the side, "Boss, I saw me something when I was in town the other day that you should know about. I seen this boy draw and kill an experienced gunfighter. The boy was so fast that the gunfighter never cleared his holster before this kid shot him dead. I told myself, 'I bet the Boss could use this ol' boy.' I just wanted you to know." Nolen mused a bit, "He was that fast, eh?" His hand replied, "Like greased lightning!" Nolen continued, "Did you get his name?" His man responded, "I never heared nobody call his name, but he should be easy to find. He wears a vest with fringes like you might see on a mountain man."

Nolen located Buckskin drinking in a seedy bar in the low-rent section of Ft. Worth. Nolen tipped his hat, "Howdy. You must be the man I've been hearing about. You're making quite a same for yourself!" Buckskin was puzzled, "You might know me, but I don't know you. What do you want?" Nolen laughed, "What do I want? I want to make money. If you're interested in making money, I think we can help each other." Buckskin raised an eyebrow, "I'm listening."

Nolen motioned to a table in the back corner, "Let's talk where we've got a little more privacy." After they sat down, "I'm Arlin Nolen. I own the Bar N. It's a little ranch south of Ft. Worth." Nolen lowered his voice, "I ain't gonna get rich raising cows on a small ranch. I need to get bigger. I need to get bigger fast! That's where you come in. I need somebody with your special skills with a gun...Let me just be real plain. I need to take over other ranches by killing the owners and rustling their cattle." Nolen paused to get Buckskin's reaction.

Buckskin stared at Nolen for several minutes. He finally asked, "How do I kill these ranchers without getting hung by the law or lynched by their friends?" Nolen grinned, "That's where I come in. I will have a plan for each takeover. Our first choice is to get the rancher to draw on you. That way you're always acting in self-defense."

Buckskin was still skeptical, "Just how do I get them to pull on me?" Nolen retorted, "Are you stupid? Were your ma and pa brother and sister? I don't think I've ever seen a sum bitch as dumb as you!" Buckskin jumped to his feet, his hand hovering over the butt of his pistol, "Mister, are you loco? I'm about to kill you!" Nolen held up both hands in surrender as he laughed, "That's how you get someone to draw on you."

Buckskin began to calm down when he realized that Nolen was making a point. He sat back down with a sheepish look on his face. Buckskin chuckled, "Pretty slick,

Nolen. Pretty slick." Nolen smiled as they shook hands, "Follow me out to the ranch. I got a spare bedroom in the house. You won't have to stay in the bunkhouse with my hands. We're gonna be partners."

Bill Jenkins was leaned up at the bar drinking a beer with his two ranch hands. A man bumped into Bill causing him to spill his beer. The man cursed, "Why don't you watch where you're going, you dumb sum bitch?" Bill protested, "Hold on there, friend. I was just standing here. You were the one who bumped into me." The man whirled around, "Are you calling me a liar?" Bill smiled, "Of course not. It's not worth arguing over the price of a beer. Let me buy one for you." The man continued to shout, "A beer don't change the fact that you called me a liar!"

The man's unreasonable attitude put Bill's two ranch hands on the prod, "Look, mister. Mr. Jenkins couldn't have been any nicer. It's time for you to back off before there's real trouble!" The man exclaimed, "Are you dealing yourself in? Are you calling me a liar too?" The second ranch hand put his hand on the butt of his gun, "Well if he ain't, I am! You are a liar!"

The man's hand flashed to his Colt. Faster than the bar patrons could follow, the man fanned three bullets into the rancher and his hands. One cowboy gasped at the speed of the draw, "Dear God!" The man declared, "Okay, y'all seen it. It was three agin one. They were calling me a liar. A man can only take so much!"

During the Sheriff's investigation, no one said anything about the shooter goading the rancher and his men. After what they just witnessed, there wasn't anyone willing to risk getting on the bad side of the gunman.

The Sheriff asked the man, "What's your name and what were you doing in here when this fracas broke out?" The man answered, "My name is Buckskin Warner. I was trying to have a beer, minding my own business when these three started in on me. Sheriff, I'm all about law and order. I'm a peace loving man. I'm sure sorry I had to shoot these ol' boys, but they gave me no choice!"

The Sheriff sighed, "This don't make no sense. A few of the witnesses said your draw was the fastest they ever seen. Are you a gunfighter? Do you make your living with a gun?" Buckskin lied, "Oh heavens no. I'm just a simple cowboy. When I can find a job, I tend cattle. You know, Sheriff, a cowboy's life is the best. I know I won't ever be rich. All I ask for is a good horse, the open range and a few cows to look after." The Sheriff replied, "Knock it off, Warner. I know bullshit when I hear it!"

The Sheriff had the sad task of delivering the bodies of Jenkins and the hands to Mrs. Jenkins. The Sheriff said sorrowfully, "Miz Jenkins, there was a fight in town. Mr. Jenkins and y'all's two ranch hands were shot and killed. I got their bodies in the wagon."

Mrs. Jenkins collapsed in horror. When she regained consciousness, the Sheriff said softly, "Miz Jenkins, I'm so sorry. If you show me where, me and my deputies will bury them for you."

Moving On

A couple of days later, Nolen and Buckskin showed up at the Jenkins place with a deed and a stack of money. Nolen stated, "Ma'am I regretted hearing about your misfortune. I said to myself, 'Arlin, this woman is in need of your help. Get over there and help her!' So here I am! I'm gonna pay you twice what your ranch and cattle are worth, just to make sure you have enough for the rest of your life."

Mrs. Jenkins was confused, "What?...I don't know...This is all so sudden. I need to think on it." Nolen replied, "Miz Jenkins, there ain't nothing to think about! If I leave here, who's to say I won't get bit by a rattlesnake or throwed from my horse breaking my neck? Take this money and count it. You won't get a better deal. Sign the deed and you're set for life!"

Mrs. Jenkins was shaking from being pressured so hard, "Well, I guess so...If you think it's the right thing." Nolen put a reassuring arm around her, "Of course it's the right thing. Say, did I tell you how much you look like my mother?" Mrs. Jenkins signed the deed and Buckskin signed as the witness. Nolen grinned as he snatched back the money, "Buckskin." Buckskin shot the widow through the heart. Nolen said, "Let's go bury her where nobody can find her." Buckskin laughed, "Slick, real slick."

The Sheriff shook his head in disbelief. He told his deputies, "Can you believe this? That sleazy Arlin Nolen shows up and files the deed to the Jenkins place two days after Jenkins was killed. To top it off, the deed was witnessed by that damn Buckskin Warner who was the man who killed Jenkins! Something is mighty fishy!" One of the deputies retorted, "Why don't we just go ask Miz Jenkins what happened?" The Sheriff replied, "I done tried that. She's disappeared. No one knows where she's gone."

Nolen speculated to Buckskin, "I'll tell you a spread I'd like to have, the four-sixes north of us. The problem is old Burk Burnett has a gunfighter guarding his place." Buckskin shrugged, "Why is that a problem?"

Buckskin pushed through the batwing doors at the Longhorn Saloon in Ft. Worth. After ordering a beer, he said loudly, "Anybody seen that liver-lilied coward, Jake Jackson. If he quits running long enough, tell that polecat that Buckskin Warner is looking for him. I'm sick of hearing how fast he is with a gun. I'm the fastest there is! All these stories you hear about him are lies!"

A cowboy at the end of the bar responded, "I'll say one thing for you, Mr. Warner. You got sand! It will be interesting to see what Mr. Jackson does. That would be a gunfight half of Texas would pay to see!"

Mitch had worked for Burk for over 10 years. He sat down on a chair next to Burk on the porch. Burk could see the distress in his face, "Mitch, what's troubling you?" Mitch replied, "Burk, when I was in Ft. Worth yesterday, I was having a beer at the Longhorn. This loud-mouth came in and starting spouting off about Jake. How Jake was a coward and how Jake was scared of him. And how he was faster than Jake. Now I know Jake has dealt with tinhorns all his life, but some of the men said that they had seen this Buckskin Warner feller draw. They said he killed three men before they could clear leather. Some were saying that he was faster than Jake...I figured I needed to tell someone...If

I tell Jake, he might get himself killed going after this feller. I dang sure didn't want to tell Miss Anne cause I didn't want to worry her none…So I figured I'd tell you. I knew you would know what to do." Burk patted Mitch on the knee, "You did the right thing, Mitch. You go join the rest of the boys."

Burk got up to go inside for a cup of coffee. When he opened the screen door, Anne was standing there. Burk could tell by the look on her face that she had heard everything. She begged, "Burk, please don't tell him!" Burk sighed, "Anne, we can't hide it. Sooner or later, he's gonna hear it from somebody." Tears welled up in Anne's eyes, "Pa, what are we going to do?" Burk responded, "We're gonna do the only thing we can do. We're going to tell him."

After Supper

That night after supper, Jake, Anne and Burk sat out on the porch to take in the cool evening breeze. Jake asked, "Well, is someone going to tell me what no one wants to say?" Burk said, "Mitch was in Ft. Worth. It seems some yahoo is gunning for you." Jake laughed, "Is that all? A bunch have tried it and a bunch are on Boot Hill." Burk replied, "I know. I know…Folks are saying this gunslinger is different. They say some have seen him draw and that he's faster than you." Anne interjected, "Honey, don't pay any attention to what that man is saying. Just stay here. Eventually, he'll go away." Jake smiled, "Anne, you know it doesn't work that way. The first time I let someone threaten me and get away with it, they'll be ten more right behind him. No, I'll head to Ft. Worth in the morning. This needs to be taken care of."

Ft. Worth was buzzing when Jake rode into town. People were literally running to tell their friends that the big gunfight was about to happen. Jake tied up Buck in front of the Longhorn and pushed through the batwing doors. Jake announced, "I hear there's a man looking for me, a mister buckhide or something like that. Anybody seen him?" Buckskin wasn't in the bar.

It didn't take long before a voice boomed from out on the street, "Jackson, you can't hide in there forever! Come out and face me!" Jake confidently made his way to the street. He smirked as he gestured towards Buckskin, "Surely, this ain't what all the ruckus is about. Buckhide, you looking for me?" Buckskin replied, "It's Buckskin nor Buckhide! I'm surprised you showed up! You're about to wish you hadn't!" Jake laughed, "Unless you're gonna try to talk me to death, Buckhide, draw." Jake had to admit Buckskin was fast. Fast as everybody said he was. Buckskin got off two shots before Jake could fire his first one. The bullets from Buckskin penetrated an arm and a leg. Jake's bullet penetrated a skull. Pieces of Buckskin's head were scattered all over the street. The crowd that had lined the street exploded in cheers.

Jake raised his hands for quiet. He asked, "This man was obviously a hired killer. Does anyone know who he worked for?" Arlin Nolen was standing among the spectators. He was dismayed at the outcome of the gunfight. Nolen felt a wave of fear rise up in him when a number of people pointed at him in response to Jake's question. Nolen started backing up, "Now hold on. I knew Buckskin and he did work for me. But I didn't tell him to go after you!" Several voices from the crowd yelled, "Liar!"

Jake stated, "I've seen a lot of guilty men in my day. There's no question, you're one of them." A slug from Jake's Colt put a hole where Nolen's heart used to be.

That night in bed, Anne snuggled up to Jake being careful of his bandaged arm and leg, "Honey, I know we've talked about this before, but have you given any more thought to having children?" Jake laughed, "I'm afraid that horse has left the barn." Anne replied, "Maybe." She drifted off to sleep. Jake was wide awake.

The End

William H. Joiner Jr.

Made in the USA
Coppell, TX
09 June 2020

26866355R00079